The summer she turned eleven, **Aimee Carson** left the children's section of the library and entered an aisle full of Mills & Boon® novels. She promptly pulled out a book, sat on the floor, and read the entire story. It has been a love affair that has lasted for over thirty years.

Despite a fantastic job working part-time as a physician in the Alaskan Bush (think *Northern Exposure* and *ER*, minus the beautiful mountains and George Clooney), she also enjoys being at home in the gorgeous Black Hills of South Dakota, riding her dirt bike with her three wonderful kids and beyond patient husband. But, whether she's at home or at work, every morning is spent creating the stories she loves so much. Her motto? Life is too short to do anything less than what you absolutely love. She counts herself lucky to have two jobs she adores, and incredibly blessed to be a part of Mills & Boon's family of talented authors.

Aimee Carson's first book,
SECRET HISTORY OF A GOOD GIRL,
was published in

Mills & Boon Loves…

a collection of novels from our fantastic new authors.

The collection is still available to buy from
www.millsandboon.co.uk

DARE SHE
KISS & TELL?

BY
AIMEE CARSON

First published in Great Britain 2012
by Mills & Boon, an imprint of Harlequin (UK) Limited,
Eton House, 18-24 Paradise Road, Richmond, Surrey TW9 1SR

© Aimee Carson 2012

ISBN: 978 0 263 89311 3

Harlequin (UK) policy is to use papers that are natural, renewable and recyclable products and made from wood grown in sustainable forests. The logging and manufacturing process conform to the legal environmental regulations of the country of origin.

Printed and bound in Spain
by Blackprint CPI, Barcelona

DARE SHE
KISS & TELL?

To my dog, Akiko,
who is really just a cat incognito.
Thanks for the entertaining attitude.

CHAPTER ONE

ARMS crossed, legs braced shoulder width apart, Hunter Philips stood in the Green Room at Miami's WTDU TV station and studied the woman on the monitor, mentally preparing for the upcoming clash. On screen Carly Wolfe smiled at the talk-show host and the audience. The little troublemaker was prettier than he'd imagined, with long, glossy brown hair pulled forward over one shoulder and elegant legs crossed. Her leopard print slip dress was flirty and seductively short, matching a pair of killer heels. An outfit perfect for the host's live midnight show, but mostly for visually seducing a guy into a stupor of compliance. Every man in the viewing area with a functioning libido was quite likely licking their TV screen about now.

Clearly smitten, the blond talk-show host leaned back in his chair, his mahogany desk catty-corner to the leather love seat where Carly Wolfe sat. "I enjoyed your daily blog accounts of your...shall we say..." Brian O'Connor's smile grew bigger "...*creative* attempts to obtain Hunter Philips's comment before running your story in the *Miami Insider*. Owning a network security consultant business must leave him little time for the press."

Her smile was warm and genuine. "I was told he's a very busy man."

"How many times did you contact him?"

"I called his secretary six times." The woman laced her fingers, hooking them at the end of her knee, and sent the host a delightfully mischievous look. "Seven if you count my attempt to hire his company to help with my social networking security settings."

The wave of laughter from the audience blended with the host's chuckle. He was clearly charmed by his guest, and Hunter's lips twisted in a humorless smile. Carly Wolfe's fun-loving nature had the audience firmly twined around her delicate pinky finger, which meant Hunter was in some serious trouble.

"I don't know for sure," Brian O'Connor said, oozing the easy sarcasm that made him so popular with the heavily sought-after twenty-to-thirty-five-year-old demographic, "but I imagine Hunter Philips's company usually deals with more complicated accounts than simple social networking settings."

A playful twinkle appeared in her gaze. "That's the impression I got from his secretary."

Hunter stared at Carly's captivating amber-colored eyes and creamy skin, his body appreciating the entire package. Physical attraction he'd learned to ignore, but these last few weeks he'd grown intrigued and amused as Carly Wolfe's attempts to get his comment had proved increasingly more ingenious. Unfortunately the sassy sex appeal and the spirited sense of fun was an irresistible combination.

No doubt she'd learned to use her charms to her advantage.

Despite the need to pace, the urge to *move*, Hunter remained still, mentally running through his options for handling the journalist as he assessed her on the monitor. Years ago he'd undergone extensive training, learning how to wait patiently and ignore the chaotic pump of adrenaline surging through his body—no matter the danger. And what did it say about the sad state of his life when danger now came in the form of a pretty reporter?

Hunter forced himself to listen as the host went on.

"Ms. Wolfe," Brian O'Connor said. "For those few Miamians who haven't read your article, tell us about the program Hunter Philips created that has you so upset with him."

"It's a break-up app called 'The Ditchinator,'" she said. There was a second ripple of laughter from the audience, and Hunter's lips twisted wryly. Leave it to Pete Booker, his partner, to choose an insulting name. "Voicemail, text messages, even email," she went on. "We've all been dumped coldheartedly before." She turned to the audience with an inviting smile that called for solidarity among the rejected. "Am I right?"

A rousing round of applause and whistles broke out from the crowd, and Hunter grimaced. His reason for designing apps on the side was to fight his growing restlessness—an uneasy edginess he couldn't explain—*not* to bring about a potential PR problem for his company. Especially with a program he'd created eight years ago during a moment of weakness. He never should have given his partner the go-ahead to rework the idea.

Forcing his attention back to the monitor, Hunter listened as the host addressed Carly. "Are you still interested in speaking with Mr. Philips?"

"I'm *more* than interested, Brian," Carly Wolfe said. "I'm dying to talk to him—if only for a minute." She turned her winning expression toward the audience, and her beguiling charm reached through the television screen and tugged hard on Hunter's libido. "What do you guys think?" she said. "Should I keep pursuing Mr. Philips to hear what he has to say for himself?"

It was clear from the whoops and cheers that the audience was ready to string Hunter up, and his muscles tightened with tension, like rubber bands stretched to the max.

Long ago he'd been secretly tried, convicted, before being

metaphorically hung for being the bad guy—all thanks to another beautiful reporter who had needed her story. This time he had every intention of fighting back…with any means necessary.

"Mr. Philips?" a crew member said as he entered the room. "You're on in one minute."

With the announcement of a commercial break, Carly relaxed in the love seat arranged diagonally to the host. She hoped Hunter Philips was watching the show and saw that the audience was as fired up about his insulting app as she was.

She was no stranger to humiliation—was becoming quite the expert, in fact. And who *hadn't* experienced an impersonal break-up these days? But the memory of Jeremy's insensitive Ditchinator message boiled Carly's blood. If he'd simply broken it off with a quick text message she would have been over him in about forty-eight hours. Okay, probably less. The way she'd learned Thomas had dumped her—via a newspaper article and, worse, to save his financial bottom line—had been a theme park ride of embarrassment, minus the thrills and fun. The Ditchinator took the experience in a different direction. It was heartless, for sure. But the worst part? It was so…so…*flippant*.

And just how horrendous would it have been if she'd actually been in *love*?

There was no way she was going to let the elusive Hunter Philips remain in the shadows, raking in money at other people's painful expense.

The commercial break over, the host said, "We were lucky to receive a surprise phone call today. Ms. Wolfe, you're about to get your wish."

Carly froze, a strong sense of foreboding and inevitability curling in her chest, and she forgot to breathe as the host went on.

"Ladies and gentlemen, please welcome to the show the creator of The Ditchinator—Mr. Hunter Philips."

An electric flash zapped Carly's every nerve, leaving her body numb. *Great*. After chasing Hunter Philips for weeks, he'd trumped her maneuvers by turning up when she was most unprepared. Crafty little devil.

Stunned, and irritatingly impressed by his move, Carly felt her heart hammer, and she forced herself to breathe as the man appeared, heading toward her amid the audience's applause. He wore dark pants and a classy black, long-sleeved knit shirt that hugged a chest too delicious to contemplate. Talk about feeling unprepared. Delectable torsos could definitely prove to be a distraction.

His dark hair was short on the sides, with just the right amount of thickness on top. His tall frame, replete with lean muscle, moved with a sinewy grace that exuded a lethal readiness—conjuring images of a night prowler poised to pounce.

Carly had the distinct impression she was the target.

Brian O'Connor stood as the man strode toward the couch and the two shook hands across the desk. The applause died down as Hunter Philips sat on the love seat beside her. The leather cushion dipped slightly…and Carly's stomach along with it.

The host said, "So, Mr. Philips—"

"Hunter."

The man's voice was smooth, yet with an underlying core of steel that triggered Carly's internal alarms, confirming that this was not a man to treat lightly. But after all the stunts she'd pulled, well…it was too late to back down now.

"Hunter," the host repeated. "Miami has been following Ms. Wolfe's blog updates as she tried several unusual techniques to get you to comment before she ran her column, and I'd like to know what you thought of her attempts."

Hunter Philips shifted in the seat to face her, his intense

iced-blue eyes landing on Carly. A static energy bristled along her nerves, paralyzing her. A classic "deer meets headlights" moment.

Hunter's smile was slight. Secretive. "I was disappointed we couldn't accept your social networking job. It sounded fascinating," he said dryly. "And sadly," he went on, "I wasn't able to use the *Star Trek* convention tickets you sent as an enticement to accept your offer."

An amused murmur moved through the audience—most likely because Hunter Philips was so far from the stereotype to attend such a function it was laughable.

Which was probably why Brian O'Connor was chuckling as well. "Thoughtful gift."

Hunter Philips studied Carly, his brow crinkling mockingly. "It would have been even better if I were a fan of the franchise," he said, his nerve-racking gaze pinning her down.

Mentally she shook herself from her stupor. *Now's your chance, Carly. Just keep it cool. Keep it easy-breezy. And for God's sake, whatever you do, don't let your emotions get the best of you again.*

She tried for her standard disarming smile, the kind that usually won people over, holding out little hope that it would sway this darkly dangerous man next to her. "Sci-fi isn't your thing?"

"I prefer mysteries and thrillers…"

"I'm sure you do." He was mysterious, all right. "I'll keep your genre preference in mind next time."

His lips curled at one corner, more in warning than humor. "There won't be a next time."

"Pity." Those watchful eyes made the hair at her neck prickle, but she refused to back down from his gaze. "Even though chasing your comment ultimately proved fruitless, it was still fun."

The host chuckled. "I liked the story of when you tried to deliver a singing candy-gram."

"That didn't even get me past Security," Carly said wryly.

Hunter lifted an eyebrow at her, even as he addressed the host. "My favorite was when she applied online for a position at my company."

Despite her nerves, and the smoldering anger she was beginning to feel building inside her, she tried injecting a little more false charm into her smile. "I'd hoped a job interview would at least get me personal contact."

"Personal contact is good," Brian O'Connor commented slyly.

Hunter's gaze grazed purposefully across her lips—setting off a firestorm of confusion in her body—before returning to her eyes. "I can see how Ms. Wolfe's charms would be more effective in person."

Carly's heart contracted, and her anger climbed higher as comprehension dawned. He wasn't simply checking her out; he was accusing her of flirting with intent. And the warning in his gaze made it clear he was less than amused. But engaging others came naturally to her. She liked people. Especially *interesting* people. And the fascinating Hunter Philips was overqualified for the title.

"Well…" She struggled to keep her irritation from showing. "While *you* specialize in avoidance, I'm much better at one-on-one."

"Yes." His tone held an intriguing combination of both accusation and sensual suggestion, setting her every cell thrumming. "I imagine you are."

Her lips flattened. If she was going to be accused of using flirting as a tool, she might as well give him her best shot. She leaned a tad closer and crossed her legs in his direction, her dress creeping higher on her thigh as planned. "And you?" she said, as innocently as she could.

His glance at her legs was quick but hair-raising, followed by a look that acknowledged both her attributes and her attempt to throw him off. In contrast to the wild knocking in her chest, he was cool and collected as he went on. "It depends on who the other 'one' is."

She wasn't sure if he was truly attracted to her or not. If he was, he clearly could control himself.

"I'm good with a face-to-face with someone I find intriguing and clever," he went on. She got the impression he was referring to her. And yet somehow…it wasn't a compliment. "The encrypted résumé you sent to my office was interesting and creative. The simple substitution cipher you used was easy to decode, but still…" a barely perceptible nod in her direction "…it was a genius touch that ensured it got passed directly to me."

"As one who seems overly keen on protecting information," she said with a pointed look, "I thought you'd appreciate the effort."

"I did." His tiny smile screamed *Caution! Trouble ahead!* and his words made it clear why. "Though my silence on the matter should have been response enough."

"A simple 'no comment' would have sufficed."

"I doubt you would have settled for that." His powerful gaze gave her the impression he knew her every thought. An impression made even more annoying by the fact that he was right—she wouldn't have been satisfied with that easy get-out. "And since I declined your offer of a meeting," he went on, "I'm returning the secret decoder ring you sent as a gift."

As another twitter of amusement moved through the studio audience, Hunter reached into his pants pocket and then held out the tiny object, his gaze on hers. For a moment she detected a faint light in his eyes. Despite everything, he *had* been amused by her attempts to meet with him.

Stunned, she stared at him blankly.

Hunter patiently continued to hold out the ring and said dryly, "I half expected you to show up and request membership at the boxing gym I use."

He almost sounded disappointed she hadn't.

Feeling more confident, she smiled and held out her hand for the gag gift. "If I'd known you frequented such a facility I'd—" He placed the ring in her palm, warm fingers brushing her skin, and the electric current upped her prickly awareness of him by a billion watts. Her traitorous voice turned a tad husky. "I'd have been there."

"I suspect you would have," he murmured.

Carly had the feeling the man was noticing, cataloguing and storing away every detail about her. To what dark purpose she had no idea. The thought sent an illicit shimmer of excitement down her spine. Trapped in his gaze, Carly struggled for a response, but Brian O'Connor spared her the effort, announcing they were cutting to commercial.

During the break, Hunter leaned closer. "Why are you chasing me down, Ms. Wolfe?"

The confidential conversation emboldened her, and she lifted her chin. "To get you to publically admit your mean-spirited app sucks."

He cocked his head in caution. "You'll be waiting a long time."

She ignored his response. "Eventually—" her smile held zero warmth "—I'm going to get you to pull it off the market so no one else has to suffer."

"I'm curious…" His lethally secretive smile returned. "How much of your body will you expose for your cause?"

Clearly he was trying to get her riled. She fought to maintain her cool. "Which parts would prove most effective?"

"I'm open to suggestions."

"My middle finger, perhaps?"

"I prefer rounder…" his eyes skimmed her breasts, leaving

her sizzling "…softer parts." His gaze returned to her lips. "Though your sharp tongue holds a certain appeal."

She considered sticking her tongue out at him until his eyes returned to hers—seemingly unaffected, still unerringly focused, and full of a dangerous warning that left her breathless.

Fortunately the host announced the end of the commercial. Desperate for oxygen, and a break from Hunter's maddening effect on her body, she tore her gaze from him back to Brian O'Connor as he addressed her.

"Now that you have Hunter's attention," the host said, "what would you like to say?"

Go to hell came to mind. Unfortunately this wasn't cable—no swearing allowed.

But if she couldn't speak her mind, she could at least get him to face the music—off-key notes and all. "On behalf of all those affected, I'd like to thank you personally for the creation of The Ditchinator and the message it sends: 'It's over, babe.'" In keeping with their interaction to date, she lifted an eyebrow that was outwardly flirtatious but heavy with biting subtext. "You're quite the poet."

"You're easily impressed."

"It must have taken you hours to compose."

Hunter looked as if he wanted to smile. Whether despite her insult or because of it she wasn't sure. "Only a few seconds, actually. But at least it's short and to the point."

"Oh, it's *extremely* pointy, all right," she said. She twisted on the love seat to face her opponent more directly, refusing to let him get an outward rise out of her. "But what makes the experience *super*-fun is the bulk email the Ditchinator sends, notifying friends and social network followers that you're now single and available." Her smile turned overly sweet. "Nice feature."

"I thought so," he said, as if she was being serious. But

Hunter Philips was the sort of man who didn't miss a thing, not with that disturbingly calculated gaze that bored into hers.

"It certainly is a time-saver," the host said, clearly trying to rejoin the discussion.

Hunter's intense focus remained on Carly. "I admire efficiency."

"I'm sure you do," she said.

"It's a fast-paced world we live in," Hunter returned.

"Perhaps too fast," she said, aware they were still shutting Brian O'Connor out. Hunter wasn't playing nice with the host. She doubted he *ever* played nice. And she was too engrossed in this visual and verbal duel to care.

"Care to hear my favorite feature of your app?" She threw her arm across the back of the couch and leaned closer. His woodsy scent filled her senses. "The extensive list of songs to choose from to accompany the message."

The host chimed in. "The one I'd hate to be on the receiving end of is Tchaikovsky's *Nutcracker*," he said with an exaggerated shiver, clearly for the benefit of an amused audience.

She looked past Hunter to address Brian O'Connor, her tone laden with sarcasm. "Mr. Philips *is* very clever, isn't he?" Her eyes crash-landed back on Mr. Ditchinator.

"Hunter," the man insisted, his gaze trained on her. "And *your* ex-boyfriend's choice of songs?"

"It was an extra-special title. 'How Can I Miss You When You Won't Go Away?'"

Though the audience gasped and snickered, Hunter Philips didn't register the musical slight, and Brian O'Connor said, "Obscure. But effectively rude."

"Which leaves me curious as to why Ms. Wolfe is using her column in the *Miami Insider* to target me," Hunter said.

Hunter faced Carly again. Though braced for the impact, she felt the force of his gaze to her core.

"You don't seem particularly angry at the man who sent you the message," he said smoothly. "Your ex-boyfriend."

"We hadn't been together long," she said. "We weren't seriously involved."

His eyes held hers as he tipped his head. "I find that hard to believe."

"Why?"

"'Hell hath no fury' and all..."

Suddenly she realized he'd turned the tables and the attack was now on *her*. Subtle, so as to not raise the crowd's ire, but there nonetheless. The insinuation increased the tension in the air until it was almost palpable, and their host remained silent, no doubt enjoying the show they were providing.

But Carly let Hunter know with a small smile that she was on to his game. "This isn't a scorned woman's vendetta."

"You haven't flipped the coin from love to hate?" Hunter said.

"Love is one emotion I've yet to experience," she said. Although she'd come close once.

"I'm sorry to hear that."

"Oh?" She feigned surprise. "Does that lessen the fun of your app for you?"

He was clearly biting back a smile. "Not at all."

"Or is it entertaining simply to use your program to dump all your girlfriends?"

"I don't sleep around," he said.

Her brow bunched at his tone. Was he implying *she* did?

"I'm more..." He paused, as if searching for the right word. But she knew it was all for show. "*Prudent* in my choices."

If her lips pressed any tighter at the obvious dig they would merge into one.

The light in his eyes was maddening. "Nor am I vindictive when it ends."

She longed to knock the coolly lethal, amused look from

his face as he continued to bait her. "Trust me," she said. "*If* I'd wanted vengeance against my ex, I would have taken it out on him—not you."

"So why the need to lay your break-up at my feet?"

"It wasn't getting ditched that bothered me." Heart pounding under his scrutiny, she barely restrained the anger that begged to be unleashed. She held his gaze. "It was the method in which he chose to do it. And *you* created the app."

"Yes, I did," he said smoothly.

Her irritation rose. Damn it, his response was so deviously *agreeable*. His simple, matter-of-fact confirmation knocked her accusation to the ground, leaving it less effective. And he *knew* it. "My boyfriend was simply an insensitive coward. You, however," Carly said, her voice low, hoping for a loss of his tight control when faced with the brutal truth, "are exploiting people's callous treatment of others simply to make money."

The worst of the worst. A bottom-feeder, as far as Carly was concerned.

There was no flicker of emotion in Hunter's cool, hard gaze—just like Thomas after he'd dumped her to save himself. Hunter's I'm-in-control smile was infuriating. And right now he was the poster boy for every unpleasant break-up she'd ever experienced.

"Unfortunately," he said, "human nature is what it is." He paused before going on, a single brow arching higher. "Perhaps the problem is you're too naive."

Resentment burned her belly, because she'd heard that before—from the two men who had mattered most. Hunter Philips was a member of the same heartless club as her father and Thomas—where ruthlessness ruled, money was king and success came before all else.

Her sizzling fuse grew shorter, the spark drawing closer to her heart, and words poured out unchecked. "That's a rotten excuse for fueling man's sprint toward the death of human decency."

The words lingered in the stunned silence that followed, and Carly cringed.

Just perfect, Carly. A nice over-the-top histrionic retort, implying you're a crazy lady.

She'd let her emotions get the best of her…again. *Jeez,* hadn't she learned anything in the last three years?

Hunter's relaxed posture remained in place. His eyes were communicating one thing: her wild words were exactly what the infuriating man had planned. "Are you saying I'm responsible for the downfall of human decency?" The lines in his brow grew deeper. "Because that's a pretty heavy accusation for one frivolously insignificant app," he said, and then he turned his small smile toward the audience, drawing them in. "If I'd known how important it was when I designed it, I would have paid more attention."

A ripple of amusement moved through the crowd, and she knew her role in the show had just gone from lighthearted arts and entertainment reporter to bitter, jilted ex—with a generous dose of crazy.

Hunter returned his gaze to her, and frustration tightened its fist on her heart. There was such a feeling of…of…*incompleteness* about it. He'd swooped in, deciphered her like the easy read she was, and figured out just which buttons to push. He was more than an unusually cool, good-looking computer expert—his demeanor was a killer mix of cunning arctic fox and dangerous black panther. Obviously this was no simple network security consultant.

So why had Hunter designed such a personal app? The facts didn't square with the self-controlled man she'd just engaged in a battle of wits. Carly coming in last, of course.

"Unfortunately we're running out of time," the host said, disappointment in his voice.

Hunter's gaze remained locked with Carly's—a gut-twisting, heart-pounding moment of communication from victor…to loser.

"Too bad we can't come back again," she said provocatively, and held Hunter's gaze, hurling daggers meant to penetrate his steely armor, but sure they were being deflected with ease. "I'd love to hear what inspired the creation of The Ditchinator."

For the first time a hard glint flickered in his eyes—a look so stony she had to force herself not to flinch.

The host saved the day. "I would too." He turned to the audience. "Would you like to hear the story?" The audience went wild, and Brian O'Connor became Carly's newest BFF. "You up for it, Carly?"

"Definitely." She turned her attention back to Hunter, her tone silky, as it always was when she tried to control her anger. "But I'm sure Mr. Philips is too busy to participate." Although he hadn't moved, was as coolly collected as ever— God, she wished she had his control—he had to be mentally squirming as he searched for a way out. The thought was much more satisfying than near-miss daggers, but her fun ended when he shocked her with his answer.

"I'm game if you're game," Hunter said.

CHAPTER TWO

A SECOND show. Why had he agreed to a second show?

After a brief conversation with Brian O'Connor's producer, Hunter strode toward the TV station exit, ignoring the corridor walls filled with photos of previous guests as he homed in on the glass door at the end. He'd set himself a task, achieved his goal and won. Carly Wolfe had fought the good fight, but her anger had gotten the better of her. So Hunter should be walking away in triumph. Done. The issue behind him.

But when the talk-show host had mentioned returning, Hunter had looked at Carly's amber-colored eyes that had sparkled with challenge, the high cheekbones flushed with irritation, and he'd hesitated. Her quick-fire responses laced with biting sarcasm were entertaining. And when she'd flashed him her delightfully unique blend of charm-and-slash smile, daring him to a second go around, he'd been driven completely off course. What man wouldn't be captivated by the winningly wily Carly Wolfe—especially after her cheeky crossing-of-beautiful-bared-legs attempt to trip up his focus?

He wasn't worried he'd lose their second round of verbal tag, or that he'd succumb to her allure, because touching her was out of the question. The sexy firebrand was a problem, but one he could comfortably control—because he'd lived with a pretty reporter once, and to say it hadn't ended well was a gross understatement…

There was no better education than a negative outcome. Although with Carly around the view was admittedly five-star.

He heard Carly say his name, interrupting his thoughts, and looked to his left, appreciating her lovely face as she fell into step beside him.

Heels tapping on the wood floor, she struggled to keep up. "Interesting how you were too busy to give me five minutes of your time." The smile on her face didn't come anywhere near her eyes. For one insane moment he missed the genuine warmth she'd exuded early in the show. A warmth that had ended the moment he sat down beside her. "Yet here you are, going out of your way to come on this program, Mr. Philips."

"Hunter," he said, ignoring her enticing citrus scent.

She shot him a you-can't-be-serious look and stretched those beautiful legs, clearly determined to match his stride. "Why do you keep insisting on the use of your first name? To pretend you have a heart?"

Biting back a smile, he trained his gaze on the exit door, feeling a touch of guilt for enjoying her reaction and her struggle to keep pace with him. "You're just mad you lost."

"All I wanted from you was a few minutes of your time, but for weeks you were too busy. Yet you turn up here and then agree to a *second* show." Her tone was a mix of irritation, confusion and curiosity, as if she truly wanted an answer to the burning question. "Why?"

"Maybe you charmed me into it."

"Aphrodite herself couldn't charm *you* into going against your will," she said as she continued walking beside him. "So why *now*?

"The time suited."

She stopped in front of him, forcing him to come to a halt or plow her over. "Saturday at midnight?" Her tone radiated disbelief. "But you must be exhausted after spending the week protecting your big-name clients from sophisticated hackers and designing those heart-warming apps." Apparently she couldn't resist another dig. "I do hope you're well compensated."

Keeping a straight face was hard. "The money is excellent."

He could tell his response ticked her off even more. The slight flattening of her full lips was a dead giveaway. But eight years ago he'd painstakingly begun the process of rebuilding his life. The main benefits of the business he'd started were financial, and he wasn't about to apologize to anyone for that.

"The real question is…" She stepped closer and the crackling electricity was back, heating him up and breaking his train of thought in a disturbing way. "How much has your humiliating app made you?"

"Less than you'd think."

"I'd settle for less than I'd hoped."

He tipped his head. "And how much would that be?"

She planted a hand on a hip that displayed just the right amount of curve. "How far below zero can you count?"

This time he didn't hold back the small smile as she tried to restrain her anger. "Depends on the incentive," he said, feeling an irresistible need to bait her further. "You can try hiking your dress higher again and see how low I can go."

At the mention of her previous maneuver she didn't flinch or seem sorry—which for some reason pleased him.

"What would be the point?" she said, and her smile leaned more toward sarcasm than humor. "You aren't the type to get distracted by a little leg, are you?"

He couldn't afford to get distracted. Getting used by a woman twice in one decade would qualify him for a lifetime achievement award for stupidity. However, his body was taking notice of Carly in every way possible. Despite the years of practice, this time, with this particular woman, he struggled to seize the wayward responses and enclose them in steel even as he appreciated the sun-kissed skin, the silky brown hair and the slip-dress-covered figure built to inspire a man's imagination.

She leaned closer, as if to get his full attention. Which was ironic, seeing as how he was struggling *not* to notice everything about her. "I'm still waiting on an answer," she said.

"To which question?" he said. "If I'm susceptible to a woman openly flirting to gain an advantage or whether I have a heart?"

"I'm certain you don't have a heart," she said, and he recognized the silky tone she adopted when anger sparkled in her eyes. "But you know what else I think?"

Hunter stared at Carly. The bold challenge in her face reminded him of how far she'd gone to hunt him down. He'd pulled his punches tonight, because anything more would have agitated a crowd that was already against him. But right now they were alone, so he wrapped his tone in his usual steel. "What do you think?"

Her lids widened slightly, as if she was having second thoughts. Her words proved otherwise. "I think you're a soul-less, cold-hearted bastard whose only concern is the bottom line," she said. "The very sort of man I can't stand."

He dropped his voice to dangerous levels. "In that case you shouldn't have dared me to come back."

Her chin hiked a touch higher. "It was a last-minute decision."

"Having trouble controlling your impulses?"

Her chest hitched faster, as if she were fighting to control her anger. "I have no regrets."

"Not yet, anyway."

"I suspect your reasons for appearing tonight were less

about convenience and more about the free advertising for your heartless app."

His pause was slight, but meaningful. "But I wouldn't be here if it wasn't for you."

He was certain she was smart enough to decode his message.

A message that must have infuriated her more, as her eyes narrowed. "If you benefit financially because of tonight, you should send me flowers to show your gratitude."

The thought brought his first genuine smile. "Perhaps I will."

The muscles around her beautiful mouth tensed, as if she were biting her cheek to keep from spilling a retort. "Orchids, not roses," she said. "I like a bouquet that's original."

She crossed her arms, framing her breasts and tripping up his thoughts. Hunter wasn't sure if it was intentional or not.

"I'm easily bored," she said.

As he stared at his lovely adversary, her face radiating a mix of amusing sass, honest exasperation and barely caged antagonism, he realized why he'd agreed to come back. It wasn't just his inexplicable restlessness of late. Despite the threat she posed, he was enjoying their duel. In truth, he was in danger of liking her—and, with all his money, it was one of the few things in life he couldn't afford to do.

He passed around her, heading for the exit. "I'll keep your floral preferences in mind."

Late Monday afternoon Hunter weaved his way through the crowded, opulent lobby of SunCare Bank. His cell phone rang and, recognizing the number, he answered without a hello. "I just finished delivering the SunCare proposal. I thought you were going to try and make it?"

"*You* have smooth negotiating skills," his partner said. "*I'm* lousy with clients."

"Perhaps because you expect everyone to speak fluent binary code."

"It's the language of the future, my friend," Pete Booker said. "And I might have crummy people skills, but I'm brilliant at debugging our cross-platform encryption software. Which I finished in record time, so round of applause for me."

Hunter suppressed the grin. His friend, a former whiz kid and quintessential technogeek—the stereotype Carly Wolfe had clearly been expecting—hated meetings of any kind. And while Hunter had a healthy ego, was comfortable with his skills as an expert at cyber security, "mathematical genius" didn't even touch Booker's capabilities. Unfortunately what Mother Nature had bestowed on Booker in brains she'd shortchanged him in the social graces, leaving Hunter the front man for their business. Still, theirs was a formidable team, and there was no one Hunter trusted more.

"But I didn't call for applause," Booker said. "I called to tell you we've got trouble."

Familiar with his friend's love for conspiracy plots, Hunter maintained his role as the straight man. "More trouble than those secret silent black helicopters?"

"Chuckle on, Hunt. Cuz when Big Brother comes to haul you away, you won't be."

"I promise I'll stop laughing then," Hunter said dryly.

"Do you want to hear my news or not?"

"Only if it's about another sighting of Elvis."

"Not even close," Booker said. "It's about Carly Wolfe."

At the mention of the delightfully charming menace, Hunter frowned as he pushed through the revolving bank door and was dumped out onto the bustling, skyscraper-lined sidewalk. "Go on."

"As per your suggestion I did a little research and found out her dad is William Wolfe, founder and owner of Wolfe Broadcasting. You know—the one that owns numerous media outlets throughout the country." Booker paused as if to emphasize what came next. "Including WTDU TV station."

Hunter stopped short, instantly alert, and people on the sidewalk continued to stream around him. He hadn't completely recovered from his mental tango with the lovely Carly Wolfe. But the little troublemaker suddenly had the potential of being a much *bigger* troublemaker than he'd originally thought. "The station that airs Brian O'Connor's show," he said slowly.

"One and the same," his partner said.

Hunter forced the breath from his body in a slow, smooth motion, fighting the odd feeling of disappointment. So far he'd thought Carly Wolfe had been blatantly frank about all that she'd pulled. Her moves had been amusing because she was so upfront in her attempts to get what she wanted from him. Unlike his ex, whose manipulations had all been done behind his back. And while there were clearly no rules to the game he and Carly were engaged in, there was a sort of unwritten gentleman's agreement—if she'd been a man, that was, which she most clearly wasn't.

In Hunter's mind Carly had crossed the line into unfair play. Because she *hadn't* had to charm her way onto the show—a thought Hunter had found intensely amusing. No, she'd just picked up the phone and called her father. Making her more of a user than a wily charmer. The disappointment dug deeper.

"The second show is the least of our problems," Booker said seriously. "With that kind of connection she could maintain this public fight forever. Enough to eventually hurt the business."

Hunter's cheek twitched with tension. Firewell, Inc. wasn't just about money and success. It was about redefining himself after his old life had been stolen from him. The pause was long as Hunter grappled with the news.

"I hope you have a plan," Booker went on. "Cuz I'll be damned if I know what to do next."

As usual, the weight of responsibility sat hard on Hunter's shoulders, and his fingers gripped the phone. But eight years ago Booker had stuck by Hunter when no one else had, believing in him when most had doubted his honor. On that truth alone Hunter's business, his success—even the contentment he'd eventually found in his new life—*none* of it would have been possible without the loyalty of his friend.

Hunter forced his fingers to loosen their grip on his phone. "I'll take care of it."

He didn't know how, but it was going to start with a discussion with Ms. Carly Wolfe.

After an unsuccessful attempt to find Carly Wolfe at her office—followed by a successful discussion with a Gothically dressed coworker of hers—two hours after Booker's call Hunter drove through a rundown neighborhood lined with derelict warehouses. What was Carly thinking of, doing an interview *here*? It was far from the upscale, trendy end of Miami, and the moment he'd turned into the questionable section of town his senses had gone on alert.

Hunter pulled in front of the metal building that corresponded with the address he'd been given, parking behind a blue Mini Cooper that looked pretty new, and completely out of place. He turned off his car and spied Carly coming up the alley bisecting a pair of ramshackle warehouses. Her attention was on her cell phone conversation.

His moment of triumph was replaced by an uneasy wariness as two twenty-something males exited a warehouse door behind her, following Carly. Both looked big enough to play defensive end for a professional football team. With sweatshirt hoods covering their heads, shoulders hunched, and hands shoved into their pockets, their posture was either in defense against the unusually chilly air…or because they were hiding something.

Their steps cocky and full of purpose, the menacing-looking duo called after her, their intent clearly on Carly, and Hunter's senses rocketed from his usual tensely cautious state straight to Defcon One: battle is imminent.

Sonofabitch.

Pushing all thoughts of confrontation with Carly aside, heart pumping with the old familiar adrenaline of a pending threat, Hunter reached for his glove compartment.

"Abby," Carly said into her cellular, plugging her other ear as she tried to hear over the garbled reception and the city noises echoing along the graffiti-covered alley. "Slow down. I can't understand a word you're saying."

"He came by the office, asking where you were." Abby's voice was low and ominous. "Things are about to get ugly."

Carly grinned at the doomsday prediction. Abby, Carly's beloved Gothic friend, colleague—and perpetual pessimist—never failed to disappoint. Despite Abby's predictions that it would end with Carly being bound, gagged and stuffed in the trunk of a car, the interview Carly had just finished with the two graffiti artists had gone better than expected. Outwardly they might resemble your basic gangsters, but their raw artistic talent had blown her away.

"*Who* came by?" Carly said.

"Hunter Philips."

Carly stumbled slightly, and her heart sputtered to a stop before resuming at twice its normal rate. Gripping her phone, she tried to focus beyond the noisy traffic and a distant call from someone, somewhere. "What did you say to him?"

"Sorry, Carly," Abby said with a moan. "I told him where you were. It's just, well…he caught me by surprise. And he's so…so…"

"I know," Carly said as she puffed out a breath, sparing her friend the impossible task.

"Exactly," Abby said, leaving Carly relieved his beyond-description effect wasn't just on her.

He was too edgy and guarded to be a charming playboy. Too chillingly in control to play the bad boy. Beyond the iced stare he was criminally beautiful, with a dangerous appeal that was so flippin' fascinating Carly had had a hard time focusing on her morning's dull assignment about a new nightclub. Another earth-shattering story to add to a gripping portfolio filled with articles on the latest club, gallery or silliest hottest trend. But who could concentrate when there was someone like the enigmatic Hunter Philips filling her thoughts?

Tonight, hopefully she could keep her mind off Hunter by slaving away on her piece about the graffiti artists. *Another* in-depth profile article her boss probably wouldn't publish.

With a sigh, Carly said, "Thanks for the warning, Abby."

"Be careful, okay?" Abby said.

Carly reassured her she would and signed off, still so caught up in her attempt *not* to think about Hunter Philips that she didn't notice the man who stepped in front of her, failing to adjust her stride. She smacked into a solid chest, triggering an adrenaline surge that shot her nervous system straight to nuclear meltdown…until she looked up at Hunter Philips's face and the whole hot mess got a gazillion times worse.

While her heart added additional force to its already impressive velocity, Hunter put an arm about her waist, pulled her around, and plastered her to his side. Carly's senses were immediately barraged with several competing sensations at once.

Hunter's frosty slate-blue eyes were trained on the two men she'd interviewed. There was an utterly steely look in

Hunter's face. His lean, well-muscled—and protective—body was pressed against hers. And beneath his sophisticated hip-length leather jacket a hard object at his waist dug into her flank.

Alarms clanged in Carly's head. She was aware she should recognize the article biting into her, but she couldn't place it.

Hunter's words reeked with cool authority as he addressed the men. "I think you two should take off," he said, looking ready, able and more than willing to fight if need be.

Thad, one of her interviewees, took a step closer, his bad attitude reflected in his tone as he spoke to Hunter. "Who asked for your opinion?"

Wary readiness oozed from Hunter's every pore. The two beefy young men looked as if they'd been in a brawl or two, or maybe fifty, but Hunter's low voice remained smooth, without the tiniest hint of fear. In truth, Carly got the impression he was almost enjoying himself.

"No one asked," Hunter said, with an undeniably dangerous edge to his tone. "But I'm giving my opinion anyway."

Thad bristled, but Marcus, his graffiti-painting partner in crime, glanced at Hunter uneasily, as if sensing the new arrival wasn't someone to mess with.

"Ease up, man. We're good," Marcus said to Hunter as he grabbed his friend by the sweatshirt and pulled him back a step. "We just wanted to tell Carly she left her recorder."

"Yeah," the other replied with an even worse attitude. "And we ain't asking for *your* help."

Carly's stomach tipped under the tension of this testosterone-fest run amok, but the vicious surge of flight-or-fight response had finally ebbed, leaving communication possible.

"Hunter, back *off*. This is Thad and Marcus," she said, nodding at each in turn. "I just finished interviewing them."

Hunter looked down at her, his expression confirming that he thought she'd just crawled out of the deep end of crazy.

She held out her hand toward Thad, waiting for her digital recorder. Clearly she was more distracted than she'd thought.

Thad, still glaring at Hunter, began to remove his hand from his pocket, and Hunter's body instantly, *reflexively*, coiled protectively tighter. Damn, did the man *ever* ease up? The hard object at his left hip bit deeper into her flank, reminding her of its presence.

What the hell *was* that?

But focusing wasn't easy with the feel of his body pressed against her, the smell of his woodsy cologne, and his hand curved around her hip.

As Thad placed the recorder in her hand, Carly said, "I'll call next week to set up a time to finish."

After a nod at Carly, Thad tossed Hunter a venomous look, and the two friends headed back down the alley toward the side door to the warehouse.

After a few seconds of watching them go, Hunter said, "You can't be serious?"

"About what?"

"Interviewing them."

"Why not?" Carly looked up at him, not sure if she wanted to kick his butt for insulting her tetchy interviewees or kiss him for taking them on while thinking they were a threat to her. Even with the touchy situation resolved, not a single one of his tensed muscles had relaxed—as if he didn't quite trust it wouldn't turn ugly. Of course, *her* senses were still very much in tune with every inch of his body.

And there were a lot of inches. All of them hard.

Her shoulder was jammed against a solid chest. The arm wrapped around her waist held his lean hip to hers, and his long, powerfully built thigh pressed against her leg. This was no laid-back, artsy type—her usual preference. There wasn't a single soft spot on him. Every part was honed to perfection. And if his demeanor during a perceived threat was any indication, in a pinch his body could be used as a weapon...

With a clarity that smacked her system into heretofore unknown heart-rates, the identity of the object digging into her side suddenly became known. Ignoring the mutinous thrill, she whispered fiercely, "Is that a *gun* at your hip?"

It was a rhetorical question, because she knew the answer. How was she supposed to stop obsessing about the man when he showed up going all action-hero on her? And just which side of the law was he on?

Without blinking, he stared at her for a long moment, as if searching for the right way to respond. And then his lips twitched. "Perhaps I'm just happy to see you."

After a split second of stunned adjustment, she rolled her eyes at the ridiculously old joke. "Only if there's something seriously wrong with your anatomy." A spark of amusement briefly lit his eyes, and she knew a comeback was forthcoming. "And forget trying to weasel your way out of my question by assuring me that there is nothing wrong with your anatomy."

His amused tone was intentionally bland. "There's nothing wrong with my anatomy."

She knew that all too well, but she was also perfectly capable of admiring masculine beauty without succumbing to the appreciation. And she hoped to heaven Hunter wouldn't wind up being the exception, because his ultra-cool aura wrapped in hard-edged alertness provided a kind of excitement no man had before. Ever.

Just remember what happened the last time you found a man intriguing and fell victim to your emotions, Carly.

She wouldn't let her fascination sway her again. She *couldn't* let her fascination sway her again. Her career was only just now recovering.

"Who *are* you?" She pulled herself from his grasp and

turned to face him, ignoring her crushing disappointment at the loss of his touch. "And don't tell me you're a simple network security consultant because by the end of that show I knew you were more. And today proves my instincts right."

He looked down at her with the intense focus that always set her on guard. "What else do your instincts tell you?" he said.

That she'd never met anyone like the enigmatic Hunter Philips. That no man had ever intrigued her so thoroughly. But mostly that he was a force to be reckoned with.

"That you could have taken those two guys down with your bare hands," she said, staring up at him, knowing in her heart it was true.

After a long pause with no response from Hunter she debated her next move. She was dying for a visual confirmation of the object that adorned his hip, and there was only one ploy she could think of to accomplish her goal. He was decidedly more dangerous than she'd originally believed, which meant she should pass on the plan. Her palms were growing damp at the thought.

Don't do it, Carly. Don't do it.

Oh...what the hell.

Tamping down her nerves, she stepped even closer, his nearness providing her with a forbidden adrenaline rush. "I think you could have taken them on bare-handed without so much as wrinkling your clothes." She began circling him slowly, not having to work hard at the sensual tone. "Not a mark on your pressed white shirt..." As she rounded his side his alert gaze followed her with a keen interest that prickled her skin. Sweat pricked between her breasts. "Not a crease in your dark pants..." She ignored his probing, assessing eyes, afraid she'd lose her nerve. "Or the classy black leather jacket..."

Heart thumping harder, she stopped in front of him and

began to run her fingers down the edge of his sleek coat, as if to feel the material. What would he do when she tried to take a look?

"Am I right?" Fingers on his lapel, she risked a glance at those oh-so observant eyes, now lit with awareness, and an exhilarating rush skittered up her spine. "Would you have delivered two right hooks and emerged victorious and wrinkle-free?" Tense with anticipation, she began to lift the edge of his coat to get a peek at his hip.

Brow creased in subdued humor, Hunter pulled his jacket back in place, blocking her view. "Maybe."

Good God, he was a tease.

She dropped her hand to her side, the disappointment intense. Damn. The more she learned, the more captivating he became—and the more she wanted to uncover.

In light of everything, an interesting possibility suddenly dawned bright. She narrowed her eyes. "Are you a former crook?" Her answer came in the form of a quizzical eyebrow. "You know…" She tipped her head curiously. "One of those high-tech, illegal hacker guys who gets caught, serves his time, and then starts a security firm helping businesses protect themselves from people like them."

Hunter leaned back against the graffiti-plastered alley wall, crossing his arms. He seemed entertained by the question. Truthfully, he seemed entertained by the entire situation. And he appeared intent on driving her crazy by not answering, along with goading her every chance he got.

"What does your gut say?" he said.

"My *gut* says there is more to you than meets the eye." Carly crossed the pavement and turned to lean a shoulder against the metal wall beside him, close enough to get his attention. Hopefully his *full* attention, without compromising her own.

She had to hike her chin to meet his gaze. Flirting with a

man your own height was so much easier. Flirting with a guy when you weren't sure which side of the law he fell on…?

She lifted a brow. "Are you going to answer my question?" Not one of those beautifully wrought muscles moved. His ready-for-anything aura was undeniably fascinating. "For all I know you're a threat I should run screaming in the other direction to avoid."

Her statement finally triggered his response. "I'm not a threat," he said.

"Then why are you packing a—?"

"I used to work for the FBI."

She bunched her brow, disturbed that her interest hadn't been quelled. And neither had his electrifying effect on her. She'd hoped that learning the truth would put the kibosh on it. Help her focus again. She should have known better.

"And why is an ex-FBI agent chasing me down?" she said.

He shifted to face her, his imposing presence no less intimidating after the truth. Just like love and hate, lawmen and criminals were just the flipside of the same dangerous coin. He said, "To ask how long you plan to use your family connections to harass me."

Stunned, she tried not to gape as a flush washed through her body. Use her family connections? Apparently he was under the mistaken impression her father was an asset to her. And any discussions regarding her dad were bound to get intensely uncomfortable.

She hiked her chin, glad her excuse was real. "Unfortunately I don't have time for a discussion. I have another interview to get to."

His previously amused expression had crossed into decidedly *un*-amused territory, making him more intimidating than before. Apparently he had no intention of letting her go so easily, and her heart sank as her attempt at escape was nixed.

"In that case," he said, "I'll tag along."

CHAPTER THREE

HUNTER sat in the back row of the old theater, empty save Carly, sitting beside him, the crew, and the three naked men on stage, dancing and singing Shakespeare to an electric guitar. *"Hamlet, The Musical!"* was unique enough, and he supposed nudity added that extra edge needed in a town as jaded as Miami. But if there was a god, and s/he was benevolent, this would end soon and he could get back to his regularly scheduled confrontation.

He shifted in his seat uncomfortably and whispered, "When are you supposed to interview Hamlet?"

Carly whispered back, "As soon as the dress rehearsal is over."

He stared at the three actors, bereft of clothing. "They still call it that?"

"They have to do a run-through in costume. Or, in this case, in the nude."

Hunter flinched as one of the male actors twirled across the stage, his male parts a victim to centrifugal forces. "This goes beyond nudity," he muttered.

Her voice held more than a hint of humor. "Wednesday I'm interviewing a participant in the Pink Flamingo's annual drag queen pageant, if you want to accompany me there as well."

He shot her a skeptical look. "What kind of reporter are you, anyway?"

"A lifestyle journalist. I do arts and entertainment pieces."

On stage, the actors formed a brief chorus line, and the image of the three naked gentlemen doing a cancan almost caused Hunter to throw in the towel and leave. "You're a little liberal with your definition of entertainment," he said dryly.

Carly leaned closer, her fresh scent teasing him, her amused voice almost…hopeful. "Are you feeling uncomfortable with the play?"

He stared down at her, not knowing which was worse: the intentionally flirty vibe emanating from her beautiful face or the monstrous scene on stage. One sight scorched his vision, and the other could leave him scarred for life.

She was a manipulator who used her charms at will, yet a part of him was impressed with her courage. A person had to be either stupid or brave to enter that alley in such a dangerous section of town. Initially he'd thought she was the first, but it was evident now that it was the second. And that hint of seduction beneath her pretense of assessing his clothes—all to get a look at his gun—had both tickled him and turned him on when it should have ticked him off. He was dismayed to realize he'd crossed the line. He *liked* her.

An unfortunate complication.

"No. I'm not uncomfortable with the play," he lied, convinced she was hoping the outlandish musical would get him to bolt. But he had no intention of leaving without finishing their discussion. Like her or not, he would protect his interests. He turned his focus to the stage, hoping he had the fortitude to stick it out. "I will, however, admit I'm more comfortable in the back alley of a crime-infested neighborhood."

"Two artistic gangsters are preferable to three actors?"

"They are when they wear clothes."

"I suppose it makes it easier to hide their weapons if they're hostile," she said, obviously amused he'd misinterpreted the men's intent.

"At least I have a concealed weapons permit. I doubt those two did. And I'm ninety-nine percent positive they were carrying," he said. Then he nodded in the direction of the stage. "That's a pretty hostile sight right there."

"Just promise me you won't shoot the actors."

"My Glock is back in the glove compartment." He risked a glance at the stage, wincing at an eyeful of a bouncing Hamlet dancing a Scottish jig. "Though I *am* tempted to retrieve it."

"I never knew network security consulting was so dangerous it required a weapon," she said.

Though her words were laced with her usual dry sarcasm, genuine curiosity radiated from her face, giving her amber eyes a warm glow, and the thrum of attraction settled deeper in his gut. Up until he'd pulled her against him in the alley she'd been just another beautiful woman he could ignore. After experiencing the dip at her waist and the soft curves firsthand, he was less confident. Since Mandy, and with the demands at Firewell, Inc., his relationships had been few and far between. Brief, superficial and uncomplicated worked best.

And it didn't get any more complicated than Carly Wolfe.

Awareness burned through him, reaffirming that his vow not to touch her again was vital.

He pushed it all aside, and said, "My day is typically weapon-free. The Glock is only in my car because I visited the firing range before work."

She shot him a look that went beyond mere curiosity. "Keeping up those skills, huh?"

Hunter's stomach lurched and he turned to stare at the stage, grateful the increase in volume of the music gave him a reprieve from responding. His weekly trips to the firing range were unnecessary, but he couldn't seem to let go of the last routine he'd maintained since he'd been forced to leave the FBI, leaving a massive hole in his life.

The sharp ache resurfaced and his jaw clenched. He enjoyed what he did now, but lately he'd been chafing at the monotony…

Carly must have decided he refused to respond to her indirect question. "Why did you leave the FBI?" she asked.

He turned to study her face. Though she was clearly digging for information, the genuine warmth he'd seen on the TV monitor that first day was back. What would she say if he told her part of the truth? There were bad parts he could share, and there were worse parts he could never divulge. In an effort to protect sensitive information the FBI had kept their investigation of him private. Outside of Mandy's newspaper article about the case he'd been working on, no other information had been made available to the public.

"Off the record?" he said.

She hesitated longer than he would have liked. "Off the record."

"I was stripped of my security clearance and put on administrative leave without pay."

A shocked silence followed, filled with awful music, until she said, "Why?"

"I was working on a case that involved a group of hackers that specialized in acquiring credit card numbers. A branch of Russian organized crime was laundering their money." He took a moment to steel himself for the words that followed. "I was accused of leaking information to the mob."

The pause was painful as she stared at him, wide-eyed. "And did you?"

The words punched hard, his stomach drawing tight with anger. He'd seen the doubt in his colleagues' expressions. The questions in their eyes. Outside of his parents and Pete Booker, no one had believed the truth—not a hundred percent, anyway. Not even after he'd been cleared. So why should *she*? But somehow her doubt took a larger chunk from his already ragged pride, and left him dangerously close to the edge. He leaned closer, and a flicker of desire swept through her eyes. For some reason the thought of a payback appealed. And there was no greater payback than refusing to answer a nosy woman's question.

"What do you think?" he said.

Carly hardly knew him, and had no reason to believe in his honor. But for one terrible moment he realized he was holding his breath, hoping she would.

"I don't know," she said softly, the tone doing little to ease the doubt in her eyes. "Why don't you tell me?"

The seconds that ticked by felt like minutes to Carly, and she held her breath as she waited for Hunter's response. The news about his past had dumped a truckload of fuel on an already burning fire of curiosity, but the impassive look on Hunter's face—so close to hers it was difficult to concentrate—revealed nothing.

And then his eyes flickered with an emotion that came and went too quickly to identify. Finally Hunter leaned back in his seat, but there was a coiled energy simmering beneath the falsely relaxed air. "I think I'll let you draw your own conclusions."

Carly stared at Hunter, quietly sucking in a breath. Damn, the man was determined to drive her down crazy lane. "What eventually happened?"

"The matter was investigated and dropped for lack of evidence," he said evenly. "After that I left the force voluntarily."

From the tone in his voice it was obvious he was done with the discussion. But his response didn't make it clear if the charges against him were accurate, but couldn't be proved, or if they were false. The truth lay buried beneath the impossible-to-ruffle gaze, and her mind kept drifting back to the hard, lethally cool look on his face in the alley.

She cleared her throat, trying to ease the tension. "Being ex-FBI must have helped your business."

He shot her a pointed look. "As much as having William Wolfe for a father has helped *your* career."

The statement was like an elbow-jab to the gut, and Carly's stomach folded protectively into a knot. Her dad was her least favorite subject, and she wished the Shakespeare-singing and dancing men in the buff *had* driven Hunter away. Clearly he didn't scare easily. The next few minutes were going to be rough.

Remember the mantra, Carly. Cool. Easy-breezy.

"It didn't help as much as you'd think," she said lightly. "My dad always insisted I make it on my own." Which she had confidently set out to do, back when she'd believed hard work alone was enough. "When I landed my first job at one of his California papers no one learned who my father was until a year later."

He studied her face, as if surprised. "That must have caused a few ripples."

"My boss was certainly nicer after he found out."

Or he *had* been nice up until she'd made an iffy decision and scandal had rocked her world—both personally and professionally. And, true to his word, her father had never intervened on her behalf...not even when she'd needed his help the most.

The pain sliced like a freshly whetted knife, and Carly clutched her armrest and stared at the stage, grateful the music was loud as Hamlet belted out his monologue, bare-assed and lifting Yorick's skull further skyward with every high note. Her father's approval had always felt unattainable. But if she earned her current boss's confidence, and a little leeway to choose her stories again, she'd regain a bit of the dignity she'd lost after her mistake.

"California is a long way away," Hunter said when the

music died down. "Your dad must have been happy you were hired on at the *Miami Insider* and moved back to town."

Carly bit back a bark of humorless laughter, staring at the stage. "You would think so," she said. "But you'd be wrong. My father thinks a weekly online paper will fail. He's convinced I made a disastrous career move."

Or, more accurately, a *second* disastrous career move. As always, his lack of confidence in her rankled. But after his prediction she wouldn't leave even if the *Miami Insider* did take a nosedive at perilous speeds. She was hell-bent on proving her dad wrong.

"As a matter of fact—" Carly sent Hunter a wry smile "—he's probably eagerly waiting for the paper to fold just so he can be proved right."

Hunter narrowed his eyes skeptically. "You're saying your father had nothing to do with you winding up on Brian O'Connor's show?"

This time there was no holding back the harsh laugh. The suggestion was so absurd it hurt. "My father would never show me that kind of favoritism."

"Seems a big coincidence we ended up at the very station your father owns."

"He had nothing to do with it. I contacted the producer of the show—"

"Who wouldn't have given you the time of day if not for the family name."

She wasn't so foolish as to deny it. "Okay, so that part is true." Having the last name Wolfe had to be good for something, because the parental aspect wasn't so hot. "But Brian O'Connor is a fan of my column and was on board with the idea from the start."

"On board for what?" he asked dryly. "Ganging up on me?"

She blew out an exasperated breath. "You handled us as

easily as you handled Thad and Marcus. And you know," she said, fed up with the entire conversation as she twisted in her seat to face him, "I asked to come on Brian's show simply to state my beef with your app. *You* weren't even supposed to be there."

His brow creased with suppressed amusement even as his eyes remained unyielding. "Too bad for you I showed up."

Carly's lips pressed flat as she remembered how he'd goaded her into losing her temper. Was that his intention now?

His intense gaze was relentless as he went on. "I want you to end this public dispute."

"Well, I want you to admit The Ditchinator sucks."

"Fine. I admit it."

She shook her head. "Not good enough. Which is why I'm so pleased you agreed to a second show." She sent him her best winning smile—the one that flirted at the possibility for more. "You can go on air to admit it sucks *and* share the inspiration behind your app."

He leaned close again, a spark of awareness in his gaze that sabotaged her smooth-talking abilities. "I won't do either," he murmured silkily.

Desire constricted her throat, making breathing difficult. She knew he was attracted to her, and God knew he thrilled her like no one had before. She could never mix business with pleasure again, but a part of her longed to know if she could ever get him to act on his attraction. "Well, then, you'd best be on your guard, Mr. Philips."

His gaze dropped to her lips. "Hunter."

Awareness pricking her skin and scrambling her brain, she repeated obediently, "Hunter."

"With you around, I'm always on my guard." His lips curled at one end. "On guard against your sharp sarcasm. The cutting words. The arsenal of charm. And…" his gaze dropped to her legs this time, kicking up her body's response, and then lifted to meet her eyes "...the intentional flash of a little more thigh."

"Come this second show I'm going to pull out all the stops to use that charm and get the history behind your app."

The hard light in his gaze set her body on fire, and his secretive smile sent a shiver up her spine as he said, "There isn't a dress short enough to pull that off."

She bit back the genuine smile that threatened. "Is that a challenge?"

"There *is* no challenge." The light in his eyes grew brighter. "I will, however, take the opportunity to beat you again at your own game."

Despite herself, she let out a quiet laugh. The man might be tightly controlled, but she sensed a playful side in him. One he kept carefully in check, only allowing it to surface occasionally to tease and provoke her. "I'll accept that as the dare that it is. So how about this?" she said. "If I manage to get the answer out of you, I win. And if you can resist me..." She sent him her most charming smile—the one that had always worked up until she'd met him. "You win."

"What's the prize?" he said softly.

Danger and desire intertwined again, leaving her body with a now familiar unsettling attraction that was uniquely his. She was traversing a very narrow line—one so thin it could double as the edge of a knife. And it was hard to focus over her heart's incessant thumping. "I haven't decided on the prize yet."

"Okay, but I expect you to keep the contest fair."

"What does that entail?"

"Leveling the playing field," he said. "No more capitalizing on your father's name as a resource. Which means outside our second show any and all Wolfe Broadcasting media outlets are off-limits in your effort to publically harass me into cooperation." The man gazed at her, his eyes no less intense in the dim light, the hint of humor dwarfed by the thread of steel in his tone. "And no more below-the-belt punches."

Intrigued, she hiked her eyebrow a little higher. "What are you going to do if I break the rules? Fit me with a pair of concrete shoes?" She leaned closer, trying to be heard over the music and desperately ignoring the sensual lips mere inches from hers. "Send me an ankle bracelet attached to an anchor and take me for a boat ride out on the Atlantic?"

His gaze was dangerously daring, lit with humor, and infused with an undeniable heat. The combination provided an edgy thrill and a sense of the unknown that shouldn't have had her so captivated.

Jeez, Carly. You really are your own worst enemy.

His smile morphed from mysterious to killer. "I'll think of something."

"Carly, you know you're heading straight for disaster, right?" Abby—doubting Thomasina friend that she was—shot Carly a worried frown as she clomped across the parking lot towards the Pink Flamingo bar. The heels of Abby's hip-length leather boots were more clunk than spike, and her black leather dress with its flipped-up collar screamed *undead.* "After your blog today, Hunter Philips is gonna be seriously annoyed."

"Why?" Irritation welled for the umpteenth time that day, and Carly frowned. "The Ditchinator just hit the top ten list for app sales."

"Yeah, and *you* just used your blog and your sarcastic wit to share your opinion about that." Abby shot her a sideways look. "Creating quite a furor, I should add."

Carly battled the bothersome regret trying to worm its way in. "It was a couple of rogue comments that started the trouble."

Abby let out a snort. "I've met Hunter, remember?" She began to weave through the noisy crowd toward the front door. "And I doubt he's gonna care *who* started the trouble. He's only gonna remember where it happened."

True. Because Abby's attire might conjure images of vampires, but who wound up resembling the real bloodsucker today? Carly Wolfe, daughter of the notorious William Wolfe, the ruthless man who put results before all else.

Even his own daughter.

She pushed the bitter memory aside and concentrated on the guilt that had been trying to hijack her all day. When a few of the blog commenters had taken up the virtual vitriolic pitchfork and called for Hunter's blood Carly's heart had sunk. *She* had no problem with tossing a few, or twenty, truthfilled sarcastic jabs in his direction, but the vicious turn of the comments had been awful.

But it was done. Time for the pesky little guilt gnats to swarm around someone else.

Carly followed her friend into the old bar. In anticipation of its fifth annual drag queen pageant every inch was packed, from the scuffed wooden floor to the sea of tables and the long bar lining the wall, crowded with patrons of all ages and walks of life. Instantly her tension eased. It was the perfect place to put today behind her.

But Abby clearly wasn't on board. "I'm worried about you, Carly." Hardcore and gloomy on the outside, creamy sensitive filling on the inside, Abby went on. "Hunter Philips is trouble."

Let me count the ways, Carly thought as she trailed Abby through the crowd. He was irritatingly sexy, intriguingly mysterious and possibly criminal, just for starters. "I just want to interview last year's pageant winner and forget about today, okay?"

"Good luck with that," Abby said as she came to a halt,

and Carly almost plowed into her back as she continued. "Because *he* might have something to say about your plans."

Her throat suddenly tight, Carly peeked around Abby. Her gaze landed on Hunter, leaning against the bar. She let out a groan.

Her day had officially gone from bad to worse.

From across the room, his frosty gaze slid to hers, landed, and claimed her attention—something the man excelled at. Her body vibrated and her heart thumped louder than the subdued music pulsing through the speakers hanging from the ceiling.

"What are you gonna do?" Abby said, staring at Hunter.

Nerves scrambling for cover beneath the force of his gaze, Carly said, "I'm thinking."

From his position at the bar Hunter stared at Carly, disappointed in himself. Even after today's blog posts, he couldn't help but appreciate the miniskirt hugging legs that had taunted him during the first show. The hot pink blouse left her shoulders bare. And her sleek brown hair was loosely pulled back, displaying the elegant curve of her neck.

"Now that she's here," Booker said from beside him, breaking Hunter's mental listing of her attributes, "are you going to go over there?"

"No." Elbow on the bar counter, Hunter kept his gaze on Carly as he answered his friend. "I'm going to make her come to me."

"How do you know she will?"

Despite today's online disaster, despite everything this troublemaker had put him through, Hunter's lips tipped up at one end. "She won't be able to help herself."

"Does she have a problem with impulse control?" Booker said dryly.

Memories of her crossing her legs on that first show and

circling him in the alley brought a faint smile to Hunter's face. "You might say that." His gaze lingered on the pretty reporter—a frustratingly fascinating mix of good humor, determination, moments of genuine warmth…and the occasional sultry come-hither vibe. "Impulse control is especially difficult when her curiosity gets the better of her or she's backed into a corner."

"Dude, she's backing *us* into a corner. After her post today my secretary fielded no less than ten calls from clients asking about the negative publicity." Booker's eyes narrowed in suspicion. "I still say the worst of those comments came from blog trolls planted by our competition."

"I think our business competitors have better things to do with their time," Hunter said, suppressing a smile, and then he eyed the lovely Carly Wolfe again. "But it's definitely time to forgo the defensive and embrace the offensive." Something he hadn't done in a very long time.

An unexpected anticipation surged, and eagerness permeated Hunter's every cell with the old familiar thrill of the chase. He was looking forward to carrying out his plan…

CHAPTER FOUR

CAUGHT in Hunter's intense stare, Carly felt her stomach rock with nerves as she ran through all her options. Leave. Stay and ignore him. Or choose confrontation.

His leather jacket was sleekly urbane, not Harley-riding-belt-and-spike. Paired with dress pants and a tailored blue shirt left open at the throat, he looked movie star classily casual. And this time when he'd tracked her down he wasn't alone. Next to Hunter a gangly man slouched unceremoniously against the counter. Despite the crowded room, apprehension skittered up her spine at the thought of facing Hunter after today's debacle. He was clearly here to see her, and ignoring him would only prolong the agony.

Because how could she interview last year's winner and enjoy herself with him assessing her from afar, producing the goosebumpy awareness he always generated?

"Let's just get this over with," she finally said to Abby.

Carly forced her feet in his direction, her nerves stretching tighter with every step. As she drew near, she managed a bright smile.

"Mr. Philips." She stopped in front of the two men. "Amazing how I keep running into you. If I'd known you were coming I would have worn a shorter skirt."

"Pity I didn't call you ahead."

"This doesn't seem like a place you'd usually hang out," Carly said. "Are you here to compete in the pageant?"

Hunter's gaze swept across the room and landed on a contestant—a drag queen sporting a figure-hugging miniskirt and a pair of killer wedge shoes even Carly would be afraid to wear lest she break an ankle. "My collection of miniskirts isn't up to the task," he said dryly. A second participant joined the first, sporting a Marilyn Manson look made of red latex. Hunter turned his iced blue eyes back on Carly. "Interesting job you have."

"I'm trying to convince my boss to expand my column to include interesting community members." Her smile grew bigger as she stepped closer. "Today I proposed I do a story on you. She said no, but I think once she watches our second show she'll change her mind." Ignoring his disconcertingly alert eyes, she leaned close, hoping to get a rise out of him. "I don't think she'll be able to resist the fascinating Hunter Philips."

His cool demeanor didn't budge. "Unfortunately she'll have to."

Carly stared at him. Was he furiously irate, mildly fuming or calmly annoyed at her for her blog post today? Damn it, she shouldn't care. All she wanted was to interview last year's drag queen winner, move past the ridiculous remorse and get her confident mojo back.

"If you're so eager for my company you could just ask me out," she said. "Instead you keep hunting me down." She finally tore her gaze from Hunter to his scraggy brown-haired friend, eyeing him curiously. He wore a gaming T-shirt emblazoned with the words *'Carpe Noctem'*—Seize the Night— well-worn jeans, and ratty athletic shoes. "And this time you brought backup too. How very FBI of you."

Hunter ignored her quip and nodded at Abby, as if he remembered her, before training his eyes on Carly. "Abby,

Carly—meet Pete Booker," he said, tipping his head in his friend's direction. "Conspiracy theorist, computer genius, and—" he held Carly's gaze as that secretive smile appeared "—my business partner."

Unwanted remorse bloomed bigger in Carly's gut as polite greetings were exchanged around her. Great, now she was looking at *two* reasons to feel guilty. Pete was cute, in a boyish kind of way that defied his description. Juxtaposed with the coiled, darker edges of his partner, he appeared downright innocent. And both men were looking at her with veiled accusation.

"I suppose your presence tonight is in response to the discussion on my blog," she said.

"Discussion? The dialogue after your post was more like a…" Hunter's voice died out, and he looked to his partner as if he needed help.

Carly knew very well he didn't.

"Firing line?" Pete suggested helpfully.

"Bloodbath," Hunter said.

"Or maybe a feeding frenzy?" his partner went on.

Hunter said, "Better still—"

"No need to go at it all night, boys," Carly said dryly. She blinked back the wave of regret that had swelled the moment they'd started their repartee, but a small resigned sigh still escaped. "That wasn't my intent."

Despite the surrounding chatter, the electrically charged atmosphere popped. Two pairs of eyes were trained on her. Carly was only concerned with one set. Hunter's.

"What *was* your intent?" Hunter's voice was deceptively soft, with the same steely tone as when he'd faced the threat in the alley. "To lose our bet?" he said.

Her smile grew tight. "I'm sure the money your app is now making will make up for today's below-the-belt punch."

"Except *now* I'm getting called by every journalist in

town," he said, and then he lifted a brow with the first hint of amusement of the evening. "And it's not my fault your efforts have shot the app sales to number ten."

"Eight," she said.

He hiked a brow. "Even better."

Oh, he knew the number. Carly's lips flattened, which made maintaining her fake smile difficult. "I should probably thank you for the flowers you sent me today, expressing your appreciation." When the delivery boy had dropped the bouquet off at work, there had been no way Carly could receive the smugly sent flowers without retaliating via her blog. "But I won't."

Hunter's eyes lit with full-on humor now. "I hope the orchid and miniature bamboo arrangement I sent was unique enough for you."

Her mouth tightened. He *would* remember her words and get it just right. Just like he'd remembered her mention of tonight's pageant. Boy, he was the first man in her life to really muck with her mojo. Carly's lips compressed further, practically blocking bloodflow now, but she managed to bite out, "They were beautiful too."

As Carly maintained Hunter's gaze the tension blanketing their small foursome reached a smothering capacity until Abby broke the spell.

"Hey," Abby said, "you two are killing my end-of-the-workday happy place." With a less than happy frown on her black-lipsticked mouth, Abby turned to Pete Booker. "I'm going to enjoy a drink at a table that just opened up. You can join me if you want. And when you say no could you at least send the message via The Ditchinator to *abby_smiles@gmail.com?*" With that, Abby headed toward the empty table.

"Uh…" An awkward expression crept up the brown-haired man's face, and his gaze shifted from the back of Carly's creature-of-the-night friend to Hunter, and then to Carly. Most likely he was trying to decide which was worse—sharing a drink with a pessimistic lady simply dressed like a vampire or the two people who were actually going for each other's throats. "Excuse me," he said, and then headed off to join Abby.

Hunter watched the two with curious interest. "She doesn't bite, does she?"

"Trust me," Carly said, maneuvering into the empty spot at the bar left by Hunter's partner. "She's all doom-and-gloom bark on the outside and no bite on the inside."

"Does she write for the lifestyle section too?"

"No. She's an investigative reporter. Me…" Carly gave a slight shrug. "I find people more interesting than facts."

"Like the renowned photojournalist turned California State Senator Thomas Weaver?"

The name cuffed her on the cheek with all the force of a full-on slap, and Carly's face burned. "You've been checking up on me again."

"You haven't left me any choice." His face had an expression she'd never seen before: curiosity. "The news media speculated you fell for the senator and gave him a free pass in your article. Is it true?"

Guilt and humiliation resurfaced, and she curled her nails against her palm. She hadn't completely fallen under Thomas Weaver's spell, as accused, but she'd cared about him. Had her actions been unethical? Technically, no. Her story had been done and published *before* they'd gotten involved. Inappropriate? Probably. Stupid? Most definitely. Because she should have avoided even the appearance of a conflict of interest. Something William Wolfe, founder and CEO of Wolfe News, Broadcasting—procreator and father of Carly Wolfe, The Disappointment—never let his daughter forget.

"I didn't fall in love." She hiked her chin. "It was closer

to a very intense like." He tipped his head in humor, and she
went on. "And I didn't give him a free pass."

"I didn't think so."

She was surprised and pleased he believed her, but the feeling of validation ended when his enigmatic smile returned.

"Did you sleep with him before or after you got his story?"
he said.

Her angry retort was cut off when someone squeezed into
the space behind her, pressing her forward…and against
Hunter's hip. A firestorm of messages bombarded her: heat,
steel and a hard-edged awareness. A faint flicker of eyelids
was Hunter's only reaction.

"And I wonder…" His voice was low, controlled, the scent
of his woodsy cologne subtle. "If I slept with you, would you
drop your little vendetta?"

Along with anger, a fierce thrill seared her veins. All from
a suggestive comment meant to provoke. Despite his words,
she knew he was too self-controlled to follow through on
his suggestion. God help her if he ever did. She struggled
to maintain a bland tone. "Depends on how good you are."

"Compared to who?"

"Everyone else."

His intense gaze held a hint of amusement. "Hopefully
that's not as many as the number of stories you've written."

"Did you come tonight to insult me?"

Someone bumped Carly from behind, pushing her more
firmly against Hunter, and he cupped the back of her shoulder to steady her. Every blood vessel in her body grew thick,
the blood forced to pulse in jetstream fashion. His hand was
warm and seductively smooth, free from calluses that would
snag her skin during a caress.

"I didn't come to insult you," he said, staring down at her,
his eyes lit with definite humor now. Was he amused by her

attempt to continue breathing despite their contact? "That's your MO, not mine," he said.

Carly stared up at Hunter's sensual mouth, the square cut jaw, and eyes that were either icy fire or fiery ice. Carly wasn't sure which. Her voice was strained. "Then why are you here?"

"I came to give you fair warning," he said.

All sorts of warnings were ringing in her head. Professional ones. Personal ones…

She knew she should reply, but the sizzling feel of his palm cradling her from behind was fascinatingly protective and yet unyieldingly hard at the same time. She finally pushed the words past her tight throat. "Fair warning?" A repeat of his last two words was all she could manage.

Brilliant. Now you sound like a stupid, mindless parrot.

His gaze scanned her face. "Maybe putting you on notice is a better description."

Her mind spun. On notice about what? That her body was turning traitor? Trumped by her own libido. *Damn.* As if she wasn't already privy to that disturbing piece of news. She stared up at him, fascinated by the restrained, coiled stillness of the body pressed against hers. Outside an electrifying gaze alive with awareness, and a hard chest that slowly rose and fell—a marked contrast to her increasingly shorter gasps—he didn't move. No swooping in for a kiss, pushing his advantage.

And a very small part of her was…disappointed.

"Notice?" she said, dismayed she was down to single-word responses.

Hunter leaned forward to speak at her ear, his voice low, her pulse pounding.

"You started this war, Carly." The shimmer of his breath on her cheek sent a fresh wave of hot prickles down her back. "I just hope you're ready for the fight."

Without warning he turned and headed off, leaving Carly reeling in the aftermath. And with the sinking feeling he'd just become infinitely more dangerous.

Saturday night, Hunter turned into the WTDU TV station's parking garage, dark save the lights hanging from the concrete beams overhead. He pulled into a space, turned off his car, and sat back in the leather seat, settling in to wait. He'd shown up early with the plan of catching Carly before she entered the studio for the show.

The thought of seeing her again wound Hunter's insides tight. He struggled with the now familiar combination of distrust, amusement, and ever-growing attraction. In the theater, her fascination with his past had been unmistakable…even as she'd questioned his relationship with the mob.

His lips twisted wryly. Carly Wolfe was an unusual woman. With her around, boredom was certainly no longer an issue. At first it had been easy to write her off as nothing more than a vindictive, publicity-driven journalist. But he'd seen her remorse over the results of her blog. He'd thought her outraged innocence during the first show was an act, but this confident, modern woman had a kernel of naivety at her core. He was beginning to realize she truly believed in what she was doing. Worse, her zest for the unusual—and unfortunately for her *job*—made her all the more attractive. He couldn't remember the last time he'd felt so passionately about something.

Before his ex had gotten her story and left? Before he'd been forced out of the FBI? The memories still felt like a vacuum, threatening to suck him down. Unfortunately there was no telling what Carly would say on the show about his app, or in an attempt to learn the inspiration behind its creation…

His insides churned at the memory. But that had been eight years ago, and some things were best forgotten. He'd been stripped of his gullibility, so he needed to do what he did best. Focus. Concentrate. And protect what was his.

The problem he'd been mulling over the last few days was how to throw Carly Wolfe off her game. She was too quick to be bested during the most heated of banter, and she had no qualms about using every weapon at her disposal. Unfortunately she was also getting harder and harder to provoke.

Drumming his fingers on the steering wheel, he remembered the mute look on her face when they'd collided at the bar. For a moment her confidence had wavered, and the confused, dumbfounded expression that had followed had been the most telling of all. Apparently the wily Ms. Wolfe was as susceptible to their attraction as she'd hoped *he'd* be.

She might be a beautiful woman, and hot enough to melt the deepest winter chill, but he hadn't suffered at the hands of his ex without taking away a few hard-earned lessons. Attraction, the electric pull between them, was something he was certain he could control. And to date it was also the only thing that had truly shattered Carly's sassy confidence.

If he had to go toe-to-toe with her on the talk show, then he was going to utilize his every advantage. If he upped his game and started *truly* coming on to her he might throw her off kilter—at least enough to keep the loaded banter, and the *questions*, under his control.

Pleasure sluiced down his spine, heating vital parts, as he contemplated pursuing the lovely Carly Wolfe. But hot on its heels was the vague impression that what he was about to do was reminiscent of the stunt his ex had pulled.

Doubt fisted in his stomach—and then he saw Carly's Mini Cooper pull into the garage and park. She exited her car, and instead of fresh and flirty tonight she was dressed to kill—namely, to kill him. And any qualms he'd had regarding his strategy died.

Her silver-sequined halter top sparkled in the light, her

tiny skirt exposed fabulous legs, and the expanse of tan skin on display was truly impressive as she headed his way. Heart pumping appreciatively in response, now looking forward to his plan, Hunter slid out of his car, shutting the door behind him. The slam echoed in the concrete garage, capturing Carly's attention. And when she caught his gaze, she froze.

Yes, he was going to enjoy besting Carly Wolfe at her own game.

Surprise, intense caution and awareness hit Carly at the sight of Hunter leaning against his car, hands in his pockets. Given his parting words to her Wednesday night, the twirl of excitement in her belly was totally inappropriate—because she couldn't afford to be less than her best.

His tone was smooth, low. "You ready for another show?"

The comment was drenched in undertones, conjuring memories of the bar, but Carly ignored the hot curl of awareness. "Interesting choice of attire for a fight." She stepped closer, taking in his exquisitely cut black suit. The white dress shirt, minus a tie and open at the collar, gave him the perfect blend of elegant evening attire with a casual attitude. "Tonight could get messy," she said. "I hope you're wearing a bulletproof vest beneath that expensive outfit."

His mouth didn't smile, but his eyes did. "I suspect it *will* get messy."

The unknown promise in his gaze left her a little uneasy, and a whole lot disturbed. What trick did he have up his sleeve? The question had haunted her since his warning at the bar, and her heart thumped as all sorts of possibilities flitted through her head.

Just don't go getting all flustered when he flashes those cool blue eyes in your direction, Carly.

"Unfortunately I left my Kevlar-coated vest at home," he said.

She resumed her walk in his direction. "Too bad for you."

"Will you be slaying me with your words or your gaze?"

"Both." She came to a stop in front of him and leaned back against the car parked beside his. "Maybe white wasn't an appropriate choice of a shirt for you," she said with a smile she hoped looked confident. "Bloodstains being so hard to remove and all."

"I know. I had to throw away the one I wore the day of your blog."

"Are we still discussing that?"

"With one difference," he said.

"Which is?"

"At first I thought you'd enjoyed the bloodbath." His gaze held hers. "But after our discussion at the bar I realized I was wrong." He tipped his head, his eyes focused intently on her. "I think the potential for such a vindictive backlash against me never crossed your mind."

It hadn't. Then again, Thomas cutting her loose to save himself had come as a shock too. But that hadn't been nearly as devastating as her father's silence when she'd needed his support.

She stared up at Hunter as she fought the depressing memories, her heart beating a little bit harder. "You know, a part of me hates that you're right. But a part of me is proud too. Yes, I'd expected a healthy online debate, not a mean-spirited, vindictive slug-fest." She crossed her arms. "But if being naive means I reserve negative judgment until I've been proven wrong, it's a label I'm willing to live with."

"The trouble with your approach is that you experience a whole lot of bad."

"The trouble with your cynical view is you miss out on a whole lot of good."

He studied her for a moment, as if considering her words, and then his forehead crinkled in suppressed amusement.

"Maybe the answer to that particular dilemma lies in whether the water in the glass at the midway mark is worth drinking or not." He paused before going on, his voice a fraction lower, bordering on…*husky*. "And how thirsty you are."

The way he was looking at her made her sit up and take notice—even more than she had when she'd first laid eyes on his casually elegant self. He seemed different. She couldn't put her finger on how, except his demeanor was less distant than usual. More approachable. With a faint hint of sensual promise that left her on edge. And she realized since his fateful words at their last meeting she'd expected him to arrive tonight with all his metaphorical guns blazing. Instead, there was a distinct suggestion of something infinitely more subtle, almost…seductive.

Worry and desire slithered up her limbs, and she tucked her hands behind her back, hoping to quiet her damp palms and now fidgety fingers.

His secretive smile was small but instantaneous. "I'm making you nervous."

It wasn't a question, and that fact alone made the tension worse. How could she prepare for a fight when she had no idea what his plans were? But a part of her knew, and her heart tripped faster at the thought even as she grew disgusted with her inability to control the excitement. A heated flush filled her body. "Was reading body language part of your training, Mr. Agent Man?"

"*Ex*-Agent Man," he corrected.

She tipped her head, giving the words consideration as she slowly shook her head. "There's nothing ex about you. You have a very natural way with your understated powers of intimidation."

"I don't believe in bullying people. I'm just very sure of the choices I make in life. If that intimidates others…" He gave a slight shrug.

She hiked a brow meaningfully. "You're very sure of *all* your choices?"

He stared at her as if the question had hit home, his face momentarily doubtful, but then he seemed to recover. "Reading people is a skill I still use every day. Interpreting body language is useful while pitching a proposal to a potential client. It can help you tailor your presentation to make the most impact."

"That must give you an advantage over your techie competition."

"And others."

Did he mean her? He took a step forward. His eyes zeroed in on her face, and her stomach tightened into a smaller knot. Which conveniently made navigating its trip to her toes easier.

"Take you, for instance," he said.

Unfortunately right now she was wishing he would, but she pushed the mutinous thought aside as he went on.

"Placing your hands behind your back is a sign you're hiding something and on your guard," he said. "Advantage point...mine."

He leaned closer, his gaze too close for comfort as he scanned her face.

"You're breathing faster than usual, you have small beads of sweat on your upper lip, and your pupils are dilated."

She suspected he was right, because her eyes were so busy trying to take in every aspect of his handsome face that they were straining mightily—refusing to miss a thing. Every sharp plane, every angular edge was heightened in the play of shadow in the light.

He said, "Advantage to me again. Because it either denotes anxiety..." the loaded pause killed her "...or desire."

Her body sizzled with heat, yet she succeeded in sounding as cool as he did. "Mr. Philips, is this a lawman's way of coming on to a woman?"

"Ex-lawman." His lips tipped into a lopsided grin that was the most delicious Hunter smile to date. "And I'm just being observant," he went on smoothly.

A wave of heat left goosebumps on her arms. Her skin resembled a cobblestoned street.

No doubt he could see those too.

"Maybe I should remind you that women don't sweat." She cocked her head when he opened his mouth to respond. "And I don't like the term 'glow' either," she said.

"What do you prefer?"

"I prefer incandescence."

Before she could react, Hunter reached up and placed a finger at the corner of her mouth. Eyes wide, Carly stared up at him as he slowly stroked the skin above her lip…curling her toes as he went. A feat she would have sworn was a myth until this very moment, but her toenails were busy trying to dig a hole into her high heels. Hunter's finger dipped lightly into the groove bisecting the middle of her mouth, slicking away the few dots of sweat that were immediately replaced by others. Her heart pumped overly heated blood that surely had her glowing by now.

Damn him, he was right. She was drowning in both anxiety *and* desire. Her breaths came in short, tight increments that sounded embarrassingly like small gasps. As she stared up at him Carly's mind ran through every reason—and there were many—why she should step away. Despite her previous attempts at flirting Hunter had hung back, watching her with cool eyes, a hands-off attitude, and that emotional wall that was always present. Only a fool would believe he'd suddenly changed his mind. And William Wolfe hadn't raised a fool.

So why was she standing here, frozen like an idiot? She knew very well this was part of some master plan he'd cooked up. Had the partners at Firewell Inc. met, given the matter consideration and then voted unanimously to muck with her mind?

His eyes crinkled in muted humor. Clearly enjoying his effect on her, Hunter said, "You're definitely incandescent now."

Paralyzed by the sensual havoc he created, breathing was all she could manage as he cupped her jaw and finally placed his mouth on hers. Carly's heart thumped in her chest as her body concentrated on the hand on her face, and the lips that slanted softly, yet insistently, over hers. The rest of his body remained disengaged. Only his warm palm and warmer mouth were involved. With just enough restrained heat to melt her tenuous reserve. Until she was kissing him back, her mind whirling from the barrage of emotions.

Doubt. Distrust. And a whole lot of desire.

Being the dominant one of the three, desire seized her in its grasp, and Carly placed her palms on his chest, frustrated by the distance. Longing to feel the hard length of his body again. Why didn't he pull her closer? Even worse, why was she mad that he didn't?

She pulled her mouth from his, her breathing labored, and stared up at the slate-blue eyes. "You're holding back, G-Man." The need to feel more was driving her on, despite the embarrassing knowledge the whole thing was a ploy. "That's no way to seduce a woman."

"Maybe my goal was to frustrate, not seduce."

Desire still pulsed through her body, but her mouth went flat, the moisture left from his lips momentarily disrupting her thoughts. "Score one for the former FBI agent and his tactics," she said, as lightly as she could.

But now she was doubly annoyed. At him for being so damn honest it forced her to confront just how caught up in the moment she'd been, and how easy it was for him to maintain his distance. That emotional wall was just as frustrating when it was a sensual one. But mostly she was annoyed at herself, for knowing all of the above and *still* being so turned on she could barely think beyond the feel of his smooth shirt, the hard plane of muscle beneath her hand.

Gazes locked, she pressed on his chest. "Your mission was a success." If he wanted to resist her efforts he didn't let on, allowing her to push him back until she'd trapped him against his car.

"Feeling frustrated already?" he said.

In every way imaginable. "Very."

"Now you know how it feels."

Why was she so ticked about his control? She ignored the crippling doubt, beat back the voice that kept telling her to walk away…and popped open the top button of his shirt. Her beef with this closed-off, enigmatic man went beyond his heartless app, now including his ability to arouse her with so little effort. And why *him*—the man whose story she sought?

It's just lust, Carly. Show him you're not afraid. Leave him shaking.

Rationalization complete, unable to wait any longer, she lifted up on her tiptoes and took his mouth, pressing his lips open with hers. Hunter didn't resist, meeting her pursuit—at this level, at least—with a rasp of his silken tongue against hers. A heated ache throbbed between her legs and she finished unbuttoning his shirt enough to slide her hands inside. Mouths melding, breath mingling, the moment lingered as Carly enjoyed the crisp hair on his chest, the firm muscle. And while the kiss seared her to the core Hunter continued to hold her with nothing more than his hand at her jaw. Palms stroking his delicious torso, desperate for more, she pressed her hips to his, to the hard thighs…and other harder parts.

Firing her imagination. Leaving her knees shaky.

Hunter pulled his mouth away and without a word, his

piercing gaze on hers, rolled to his left, trapping her between his car and his unyielding length. Bringing new meaning to the term *lethal weapon*. His well-honed physique triggered all sorts of wicked fantasies. With the shift of position she'd expected, *hoped*, for more. But Hunter simply cupped her jaw with two palms instead of one, brought his mouth down, and began to kiss her with a reserve that left her shaking with frustration even as his tongue tasted hers. His grip on her face was self-controlled, yet sensual. Demanding, yet with a protective air that reminded her of being clasped to his side in the alley.

The sound of a car motor echoed along the concrete walls of the parking garage, growing closer, and Carly pulled her mouth away. She fisted her hands against his chest as she tried to catch her breath before it became humiliatingly obvious that he'd been so successful at reaching his goal.

He had everything to gain—her distraction—and she had everything to lose—like her objectivity about a possible story. Her pride. Her job. *Again*. Even potentially…her heart.

And that was something she'd never lost before.

The rough hair, warm skin and hard muscle beneath her fists were tempting, and she longed to spread her fingers to recapture as much of the sensation as she could.

She forced her hands down to her sides. "I guess I made a mistake."

The sound of the engine drew closer, and Hunter turned his back to the oncoming vehicle, casually leaning a shoulder against his car. "Your continued fixation on The Ditchinator?" he said, his gaze on her face as he fixed his buttons.

"No. I meant I suspect I'm the one that came unprepared. All your shooting range practice has come in handy." She pressed her lips together, tasting him, feeling the lingering heat of his kiss. "With your deadly aim I could really use that bulletproof vest."

A dark look flickered across his face. "Don't bother. It won't work," he said softly, his smile bordering on bitter as he reached the last button. "Some things cut worse than a bullet."

CHAPTER FIVE

"WELCOME back, Carly and Hunter," Brian O'Connor said.

The studio applause finally died as Hunter sank into the love seat next to Carly. Was he remembering wrong or was this a different leather couch? It felt smaller. Shorter. And his position next to Carly was close enough for him to smell her citrusy scent. His body still wound tight, he hummed with vibrant energy from their seductive encounter. A planned attack, actually. He hoped the effort to fluster Carly had worked. Unfortunately it had definitely distracted him as well.

"You two have become quite an item," the blond talk-show host said with a smile as he sat back at his desk. "I'll be the first to admit I enjoy a good debate."

Hunter bit back the urge to laugh and threw one arm across the back of the couch, mindful of Carly's nearly naked shoulder just inches from his fingertips. After tonight's kiss, "debate" was quite the understatement. He kept his eyes on Carly. "Ms. Wolfe is a worthy opponent."

"As is Mr. Philips," Carly said. With a hike of a brow, she shot the host one of her charming smiles before turning her loaded gaze back to Hunter. "I'm learning a lot about the art of war."

The message was hardly subtle, and the memory of their kiss twined its way around his libido and breathed it back

to life. If it had ever died in the first place. When Carly had
gone on the offensive during their encounter it had taken all
he had to keep the moment in check. He should have known
she'd fight back, but he shouldn't have enjoyed it so much.

"What have you learned?" Hunter said dryly. "That war
is won in the attack tactics?"

"More like it's lost in a failure of the defensive," she said.

Was she referring to herself? Or him? Ironically, it applied to them both.

"If your offensive is strong enough," he said, "the defensive becomes irrelevant."

Her tone was a touch too silky for comfort. "You should
know."

He eyed Carly levelly, struggling to maintain his composed demeanor, but his gaze was probably hotter than it
should be. He sincerely hoped Carly was the only one to notice. "You're fairly skilled in aggressive tactics yourself."

Carly shifted in Hunter's direction, eyes twinkling with
mischief as she crossed her long legs in his direction. Legs
that screamed for verification that they were as smooth as
they looked. So why hadn't he seized the opportunity when
he'd had the chance? His gaze lingered a moment on her
limbs before returning to hers, and the sparkle in Carly's
eyes turned to delighted amusement mixed with a smoky
awareness that was difficult to ignore. Hunter tried anyway.

"Aggressive tactics?" she echoed with an overly innocent
smile. "Are you referring to my blog on Wednesday?"

She knew full well he wasn't.

"What else?" he said.

The sassy lady simply held his gaze and said nothing. But,
much to Hunter's delight, her lips twitched—as if she was
itching to laugh.

"Speaking of Carly's blog," Brian O'Connor said, interrupting Hunter's train of thought. "You did take a pretty good beating, Hunter."

Impatience swelled. He'd forgotten about the host. Hunter suppressed a frown, annoyed at his lack of concentration in the presence of this beautiful woman. And at the need to defend himself *again*. Not only that—this time he'd positioned himself within touching range of the sexy little troublemaker...

His insides coiled tight, the memory of kissing Carly barreling over his usual ability to remain calm. It had been hotter than he'd expected. More dangerous than he'd anticipated even after factoring in her looks and sultry ways.

The blond talk-show host grinned at Hunter. "Carly's Clan had some not so nice nicknames for you."

Despite everything, Hunter had to bite back a smile at the term. "'Carly's Clan' certainly did. And a good number of them can't be shared with your audience. Most of the commenters' choices of names aren't repeatable on TV." He turned his focus back to Carly. "But among the most creative ones I was called were reprobate—"

"Fitting," Carly interjected swiftly.

With a small smile, Hunter kept talking. "Degenerate—"

"Ditto," Carly went on.

"And a rake," Hunter finished.

"Rake?" Brian O'Connor said with a chuckle, beating Carly to the comment punch. "Who uses that word in this day and age?"

Carly's smile was genuine as the two stared at Hunter, making him feel as if he was on trial. "I don't know, Brian," she said. "But it doesn't quite suit the man, does it? Rake sounds far too..." She sent Hunter an *I'm-so-cute* smile and tipped her head. "Too romantic," she finished, and Hunter appreciated the playful look she flashed him as she went on. "I suspect Mr. Philips is a bit too cut and dried for the term."

The host chuckled and said, "You don't think he's a romantic?"

Carly rested her arm on the back of the couch. Their forearms were now lightly touching, the tips of their fingers each brushing the other's elbow—briefly breaking Hunter's focus. Carly's sparkling gaze remained on his.

"You mean beyond Mr. Philips's efficiently designed app? The one he uses to *gently* tell a woman it's over?" A murmur of amusement moved through the crowd. Despite the dig, Hunter's lips twitched. "I'm sure I have no idea," Carly finished.

But her eyes told him she did, and Hunter fought the smile that threatened.

"Speaking of The Ditchinator," Brian O'Connor said. "Today it moved to number five on the top sellers list. Carly has vowed to keep up the pressure until you discontinue the app. She's also mentioned she'd like to hear about the inspiration behind the idea. In fact all of Miami is interested." He leveled a pointed look at Hunter. "Care to share your thoughts?"

"Discontinuing the app isn't in my plans at this time," Hunter said truthfully, deliberately ignoring the mention of the story behind its creation. That was one truth he had no intention of sharing.

Clearly delighted, the host said, "Can I interest you in returning in a few weeks to discuss how you're holding up against Carly's campaign?"

Hunter glanced at Carly, who looked as if she wanted to laugh, and he could no longer restrain the smile. Since Carly Wolfe had entered his life tedium was certainly no longer a threat. In fact the excitement might very well do him in. But the thought of the two of them being through after tonight left him feeling disappointed.

"I'll accept the offer to return if Carly does." Hunter shot Carly a meaningful look. "Though I'm sure Ms. Wolfe will eventually tire of her game."

"Of course I accept." Her eyes on Hunter, Carly's tone was a heady mix of amusement, arousal…and a hint of resigned irritation. "And I guarantee I won't grow tired."

A slight pause ensued, and Hunter appreciated the mixture of emotions in her eyes—until the host interrupted.

"That's right," Brian O'Connor said with a chuckle. "Tenaciousness runs in the family genes. Carly's father is *the* William Wolfe, of Wolfe Broadcasting."

Even though they were barely touching, Hunter felt the instant tension in Carly at the host's words, and the light in her eyes dimmed a touch. As if she was preparing for the upcoming discussion to turn ugly. From his proximity, it was obvious the charming smile she was aiming at Brian was now forced.

"Just to be clear," Brian said, turning to address the audience, "there is no behind-the-scenes monkey business going on. Mr. Wolfe has never been involved in our decision to have Carly on the show." He held up his hands on display. "No screws have been applied to either mine or my producer's thumbs…" He hesitated with impeccable comedic timing. "Or to any other parts of our anatomy."

When the crowd's murmur of laughter faded Carly spoke, her smile bright, her tone light—but Hunter knew it wasn't genuine. "Anyone who's worked with my father is familiar with his strict business policy, Brian. He would never apply thumbscrews on anyone's behalf." She hesitated, her smile growing bigger, but the heart was gone. "Not even his daughter's."

Hunter's brow bunched in surprise. It was the second time

she'd said something to that effect, and he mulled over the development as the host chatted about William Wolfe's current media holdings with Carly. She remained outwardly relaxed, her demeanor easy, but the tension in her body was palpable. And though the host's comments were lighthearted, with every mention of her media magnate father her laughter grew more and more hollow. The audience was clearly oblivious, but the host *had* to sense her discomfort.

It grew worse when Brian said, "In his younger days as a newspaper reporter William Wolfe was famous for his dogged pursuit of a story. He was ruthless, even, in digging up the dirt on secret pasts and shady politicians. Your pitbull-like pursuit of Hunter, here, is reminiscent of your father."

Behind his arm, Hunter felt Carly's fingers grip the back of the couch tight even as he watched her face lose a trace of its color. "We are a lot alike," she said warily.

"I imagine your dad is pretty proud?" the host said, his smile not as warm as it should have been.

Clarity hit Hunter hard. Brian O'Connor clearly *knew* about Carly's dealings with State Senator Thomas Weaver. And the host was using that knowledge to his advantage—targeting Carly. Hunter's chest slowly constricted with anger even as he fought the emotion.

It's not your problem.

His mind scrolled through every reason he shouldn't get involved. She'd brought public scrutiny on herself, was targeting *him* using her popular blog. But the biggest reason by far? He'd traded in his need to be the good guy a long time ago. In the end his commitment to Truth, Honor and Justice—and all those other values worthy of capitalization—and his tendency to protect others...*none* of it had saved him.

"But the real question is..." Brian's grin radiated a double meaning for those close enough to see. "Just *how far* will Carly Wolfe go to get her story?"

The stunned look on Carly's face slammed Hunter in the gut.

Sonofabitch.

Carly stared at Brian O'Connor as her blood seeped lower, her chest clenched so tight it made breathing impossible. Damn, damn and double damn. The host had done some digging and learned about the Thomas Weaver Affair. Humiliation, regret and pain blended in her veins, concocting a potent mix that burned as it traveled.

Blinking back the emotion, she struggled for a light-hearted, suitably glib comment. But somehow she didn't think she could spin being accused of sleeping with a man for his story, or being fired from one of her father's newspapers, in a positive light.

She was good, but she wasn't *that* good.

Carly opened her mouth, struggling for something to say, but Hunter stopped her with a discreet touch of his fingers on her elbow. A protective, reassuring gesture. His posture remained relaxed, but the hint of coiled readiness always simmering beneath his demeanor was wound tighter than usual. It had been hard enough to calmly sit there after their kiss—wondering if he'd been affected at all, aware of him on every level. Now the icy blue eyes directed at their host were positively lethal, and a back-off attitude exuded from his every pore.

Hunter said, "What father wouldn't be proud of Carly, Brian?"

"My point exactly," the host replied, clearly refusing to back down. Both men were smiling, but the undercurrents were fierce. "She inherited the Wolfe tenacity. Wednesday's blog post proves that much. The uproar afterwards must have made you angry."

The host was clearly looking for more conflict—probably in an attempt to boost his ratings.

There was a brief pause before Hunter said, his voice smooth, "Not in the least."

Carly stared at Hunter. The fact she knew that to be a lie made the statement even more outrageous.

Brian O'Connor hesitated, momentarily looking stumped, and then he narrowed his eyes slightly at Hunter, as if sensing an opportunity. "Since it didn't bother you, perhaps you'd also be willing to share the story behind The Ditchinator?"

"Absolutely," Hunter said.

Carly's heart stumbled in her chest, and Brian O'Connor's eyes zeroed in on Hunter like a laser. The switch in his focus wasn't lost on Carly. Everything Hunter did was deliberate, and now was no exception. He'd purposefully placed himself between the host and Carly.

Protecting her...again.

The host's smile was clearly self-serving. "We'd all love to hear how your app got its start."

Hunter's ultra-cool demeanor and hard-edged alertness didn't diminish as he settled deeper into the couch, as if getting comfortable before beginning his tale. "It began where all good break-up apps begin, Brian." The secretive smile was back, and Hunter's control was firmly in place. "It started when I got dumped by the woman I loved."

Late Sunday evening, fingers curled around the leather rim of a newly purchased cowboy hat, Carly stood just inside the upscale boxing gym, empty save the two men in the ring. Hunter lightly bobbed and weaved in a circle around his opponent, his face obscured by protective headgear. His movements were light. Graceful. And the sheen of sweat on his naked torso only added to the moment of pure masculine beauty. His chest was nice to touch, but the visual was a sight she might never recover from.

She loved a well-dressed man, and Hunter knew how to play that card well. But he wore the silk shorts and athletic shoes with ease too. Hunter's sparring partner was heavier, but Hunter had the advantage of speed, agility and a calculatingly cunning patience. With every swing of his opponent's arm Hunter ducked, his reflexes lightning-quick. With a sharp jab, his fist snapped against his opponent's headgear. The two circled, ducked, successfully landed hits, and the dance continued. It was Hunter in his most elemental form. And it was magnificent.

Focus, Carly. Just focus.

She sucked in a breath, trying to concentrate on the task at hand. Since Hunter's startling on-air confession and his abrupt departure when the show was over she'd been struggling to make sense of it all. She felt stunned. Dazed. Never had she met a man with such a conflicting mass of mixed messages. When the going had gotten rough, her father had remained silent. Thomas, her boyfriend, had cut her loose to save himself. Yet Hunter, the man she was at odds with, had sacrificed his privacy to protect her.

In the ring, the two men finished, a double fist-bump signaling the end of a well-matched round. Hunter's opponent ducked between the ropes, hopped off the platform, and headed past her toward the front office, nodding on his way by. Seemingly oblivious to her presence, Hunter pulled off his headgear and picked up a towel draped in the corner, using it to wipe his face.

Gathering her courage, she took a deep breath, inhaling the smell of leather tinged with a hint of sweat. "I brought you a gift." White cowboy hat in hand, she approached the ring. Hunter slowly turned to face her, the hair on his forehead damp, sexily mussed from the headgear. As she drew closer, he leaned on the top rope, looking down at her.

"How did you find me?" he said.

"You told me the first day we met you belonged to a boxing gym. It wasn't hard to figure out which one." She held the hat in his direction. "This is for you."

He glanced at her offering. "You got the truth. You won the bet," he said. "No need to give me a consolation prize."

"It's not a consolation prize."

"Then what is it?"

"It's a simple thank-you gift." She stepped forward to the edge of the ring, the hat still extended up in his direction. "You asked me before if I believed you were falsely accused of leaking information. Now I can say unequivocally that I do." His expression was careful, his blue eyes cautious. He didn't respond, or take the hat, but behind his guarded look she saw the truth—even if he wouldn't confirm it out loud. She stared up at him and dropped her arm, asking the question that had been haunting her since his actions on the show. "Why did you do it?"

She knew the answer, but she wanted to hear it from Hunter. After all his talk about his business, his priorities, and the rest of the rubbish he'd said he believed in, his good deed proved otherwise.

"It seemed like a good way to get you off my back," he said simply.

Twenty-four hours ago she would have believed him. Now she shook her head. "Liar," she said. "That's not why you offered up your confession."

If you could call it that. His account of his break-up had been sweet and simple—laced with a no-nonsense attitude and summed up in a mere four words. He'd loved. He'd lost. But even as he'd coolly stated the facts Carly had sensed the part that he wasn't sharing. He'd fooled the audience, even the host, but Carly had seen in his eyes what the others hadn't. A part of him was *still* recovering, and the fact that he'd offered up the truth, all in the name of saving her, had been humbling.

When he didn't respond, she said, "You didn't give many details about your break-up, but it was good enough to distract the host." Several heartbeats passed, still with no reply, so she went on. "You did it to draw Brian O'Connor off my case, didn't you?"

The enigmatic smile returned. The ever-elusive look in his eyes was going to drive her to insanity—which, at this point, would essentially constitute circling the crazy block. Because she'd already arrived there courtesy of the lovely sight of a shirtless Hunter.

He bent over, stepped between the ropes and hopped down, landing in front of her. "Maybe," he said as he took the hat.

"Cut it out, Mystery Man." She propped a hand on her hip, doing her best to ignore the beautiful chest on display, the lean torso replete with muscle. "I'm getting you all figured out. You were falsely accused of leaking information and went on to start a company dedicated to helping people protect theirs. I think that's a great story. One that the public would be interested in hearing."

The look he shot her was sharp. "My life really isn't that interesting." And then, as if declaring an end to the issue, he turned and headed for the locker room.

Carly followed, heels clicking on the wood floor. "We obviously have different definitions of the word."

"Aren't you tired of me yet?"

"Not even close."

Hunter kept walking, his back to her. "Are you planning on joining me in the shower?"

"If I have to."

Hunter pivoted on his heel and Carly stopped short. For the first time his expression was a mix of curiosity, amusement, and a whole load of impatience. "Do you ever *stop* being the reporter?"

"No," she said, the answer easy. "I can't stop being who I am any more than you can." She crossed her arms, feeling the truth of her words. "I'm a journalist at heart. It's not just my nature, it's my *passion*. Just like being the white-hat-wearing protector is yours, despite the fact you quit the FBI." Even as she said the words she knew the truth. One way or another he must have felt he had no option. Carly dropped her voice an octave. "You were cleared, so why *did* you leave?"

A shadow crossed his face, and the silence that stretched between them was loud—until Hunter finally said, "That nosy nature of yours must have gotten you into a lot of trouble during your life."

"That's not an answer."

"It was simply time to move on."

Carly let her expression say it all. "I'd bet my brand-new Mini Cooper you didn't *want* to leave."

The moment lasted forever as he stared at her, and when he spoke his words surprised her. "The day before we were scheduled to take our first vacation together I came home and found Mandy had packed up her stuff and gone." He paused, as if letting her adjust to the change in topic. "I had an engagement ring in my pocket."

At the words *engagement ring* Carly's heart constricted so tight it was hard for it to keep pumping. It wasn't the answer to the question she'd asked, and his attempt to distract her was obvious, but she could no more change the subject back than she could stop asking questions. He'd cranked up her curiosity, exceeding her lifetime limit to the max.

Cowboy hat in hand, he leaned back against the door leading to the locker room. "After three months of living together it was to be our first trip, and I started with dinner plans at a restaurant she'd always wanted to try. It was too expensive for a government man on a government salary, but I figured it was worth it," he went on. "Because a guy only gets married once."

Once. The assumption brought the threat of tears, burning her eyes, surprising her. When Hunter Philips made a promise, he kept it.

"When I called Mandy from work to tell her where I was taking her she must have guessed what was coming." He shrugged his shoulders. "I suppose it was easier to say no by leaving than refuse me to my face."

She blinked back the sting in her eyes. No one should be dumped in a way so cowardly and cruel—especially when he'd been about to make the ultimate commitment. "What did you do?"

His voice was easy, smooth, but the words hit hard. "I got drunk and stayed that way."

It was hardly the response she'd expected.

He tipped his head, his cool eyes steadily holding hers. "After a week-long alcohol binge that probably should have killed me, Booker finally showed up, dragged me off the couch, and shoved me in a shower with my clothes on." Face composed, he folded his arms, hat dangling from his fingers. A faint smile of memory crossed his face. "It's all a little fuzzy, but I remember yelling at him to turn off the faucet." He cut her a dry look. "Unlike Florida, the middle of a Chicago winter means the water is frigid. But Booker just held me under the spray, and I was too drunk to push back."

The reedy stature and little-boy face of Hunter's friend made the whole thing hard to picture. Not with the physical state Hunter maintained. "I can't imagine your partner effectively fighting you back."

"Like I said," he said. "I was plastered out of my mind and my coordination was bad. Of course alcohol does have the advantage of being an excellent anesthetic as well." There was a slight pause, and he hiked a self-mocking brow. "The only problem was it kept wearing off."

Though his face was composed, his gaze calm, his tone said it all.

"What happened after the cold shower?" she said.

"I sobered up enough to get into dry clothes and sat shivering on the couch, yelling at Booker to get out. He wouldn't leave." He looked at Carly, his words matter-of-fact. But his face reflected a moment that was clearly seared in his memory, earning Pete Booker the title of faithful friend for life—till death did they part. "After about an hour of angry silence from me, Booker told me I needed to stop letting Mandy's defection get to me and start doing something productive, like fight back," he said, steadily holding her gaze.

The next step was easy to guess. "And that's when The Ditchinator was born."

"To keep me busy."

"And get back at Mandy?"

"An outlet for my frustrations." A rueful smile curled on his lips. "Booker helped me work on the program. It was originally designed for email. When vacation time was over and I had to go back to work he showed up at the end of each day and we kept adding features, making it more elaborate. We spent a month on the songs alone, each trying to outdo the other by finding the best tune to go with the message." The tension in his body eased a bit. "Every time I slipped back into my black funk Booker would find another song title that made me laugh. Soon we had so many we decided to list them all as options."

There was a long pause as Carly stared at him, sensing there was more to the story that he wasn't sharing.

"And now that the app is so popular you're laughing all the way to the bank."

"Trust me," he said wryly, a brief shadow crossing his face, "no laughing is involved." He cocked his head, his expression easing a touch. "But I'll take the money, nonetheless."

There was a long pause as they stared at each other. In some small way it must provide him with a satisfying sense of comeuppance. No wonder he refused to take it off the market. But this wasn't the time to discuss her thoughts on that subject again.

Hunter unfolded his arms, providing a better view of his delicious chest. "That's it, Carly." His eyebrow arced higher. "Now you know enough of the gritty details to satisfy even *your* inquisitive nature." He looked down at the white hat in his hand before lifting his gaze to hers, his tone reflecting that he was done with the conversation. "I appreciate the gift, but it's time to call it a night."

Though his expression was still coolly collected, his eyes sizzled with a teasing heat that set her heart racing as he went on. "Unless you're really going to follow me into the shower…" He paused, letting her fill in the blank, and then turned and pushed through the door.

And as it slowly closed in her face she stared at the sign. Men's Locker Room. Body on fire, she bit her lip with a frown. Damn him for being the action-hero defender, an honorable guy who was impossible not to like. Damn him for being so darkly guarded, inflaming her curiosity with his secretive air. And damn him for his well-honed chest paired with an unflappable composure—for provoking her with his teasing words and the sexy look in her eyes…and then walking away.

Heart pounding, she let a full minute tick by as she tried to decide what to do next.

Go home now, Carly. You're done.

But what would happen if she finally called his bluff? She longed to know what he'd do if she challenged him on his sizzling words paired with a frustrating reserve. If she pushed him, would he finally lose a little of that control?

Let it go, Carly. You're done.

She bit her lower lip, staring at the locker room sign, the distinct feeling of *un*doneness leaving her feet stuck to the floor, unwilling to leave. Several agonizing moments passed, but ultimately her curiosity was her undoing. Lips pressed in a determined line, the whisper of desire growing louder, Carly pushed open the door and stepped inside.

CHAPTER SIX

AT THE back of the locker room Hunter pulled out his duffel bag and shut the locker harder than he'd planned. The slam of the metal door echoed off the sea of pristine white tile. Mind churning, he set his bag on one of several long wooden benches, burning with a mix of emotions caused by reliving old memories. And by dealing with the beautiful, *determined* Carly Wolfe.

Annoyed with himself, he pulled out his towel and clean clothes, tossing them all on the bench. After shedding his clothes and shoes, he entered one of the shower stalls separated by chest-high tiled walls.

The sting of hot water felt good, easing his aching muscles and a bit of his tension as he shampooed his hair. He wished the soap could wash the troublesome journalist from his life as easily.

When the sound of footsteps came, Hunter glanced over the wall of the shower stall. Carly appeared, rounding the last row of lockers. Hunter's heart pumped hard and his hands stilled in his soapy hair.

As if she belonged in the male domain, she came closer and stopped on the other side of the low wall. The partition was just high enough to block her view of the lower part of his body. A part that was responding to her presence, her bold maneuver, and leaving his every cell crackling with electricity.

Which brought him to the main reason he'd agreed to go back on the show again. He couldn't lie to himself anymore. He'd duped himself into thinking it was all about his boredom with a job that left him unsatisfied. He could no longer deny the *biggest* reason he was unable to walk away from her—despite all the reasons he should.

Desire. Want. *Need.*

A longing so intense it was disturbing.

And he didn't want her here, testing his ability to keep the lessons of the past in mind. Proving that with every outrageous move by Carly Wolfe those lessons were getting harder and harder to remember.

Frustrated, Hunter stuck his head under the shower, rinsing out the rest of the shampoo. His gut tensed as he debated what to do with the woman who was driving him insane. Wishing she'd leave. Ignoring the small part of him that was hoping she wouldn't.

Finished, he turned his back to the spray, careful to keep his tone level. "Are you here just to watch or to seduce a story out of me?"

Her lips tightened at his slur. "As I recall, it was you who came on to me in the parking garage."

Despite everything, a wry smile crept up his face. He wasn't particularly proud of that moment, but it had certainly been memorable. And having her just a short wall away from his naked body wasn't making this conversation easy. His blood was enthusiastically lining up on its way to a part of him that was paying close attention. *Very* close attention. "I'm not even sure it was effective."

"Oh, it was effective." She propped her hand on her hip. "And if I turned the tables and tried the tactic on you? Would it work too?"

The question lit the fire that he'd fought so hard to keep banked. The sound of water hitting tile filled the room as he debated how to respond. For some reason he couldn't stop pushing her. Testing her. "Depends on how good you are." He nodded in the direction of the condom machine on the wall, multiple Kama Sutra pictures displayed on its front. "And how many of those positions you're familiar with."

Carly glanced at the dispenser, her eyelids flickering briefly in surprise at the images. It took a moment for her to respond. "I'm familiar with the first and the third." She turned to meet his gaze again, her tone dry. "Number five is physically impossible." After a pause, the sassy confidence was fully back in place and she stepped closer, folding her arms on the tile wall, eyes lit with challenge. "But I'm willing to try number four with you."

Heat surged, and he fought the smile. He knew what the little minx was up to, and he felt a punishing need to see if she would actually follow through. Almost as strong as the punishing need coursing through his body now. "Here?" He lifted a brow. "Now?"

For the first time her gaze dropped below his waist. "Why wait?"

If he got any harder he'd crack. "It's your call," he said, and counted out the pounding heartbeats.

Her pink tongue touched her lips, either in nerves or anticipation—or both—and her breaths came faster. "Got any quarters for the machine?"

"Side pocket of my gym bag."

Hunter waited, wanting to see just how far the bold woman would go. Knowing that this time pulling back would be impossible…

Heart thumping from their exchange and intense longing, Carly glanced at the condom dispenser again, conflicted.

She wasn't supposed to be here—not when she'd been trying to convince her boss to let her do a story on Hunter. She'd been refused each time, but sleeping with him now would still be stupid. Massively stupid. Yet, despite that knowledge, she was still torn between what she should do—which was retreat from the challenge—and what she wanted to do...

She cut her gaze to Hunter, forcing herself *not* to inspect the entire package again and risk a total meltdown. Arms crossed, water sluicing down his back, he regarded her with more than just desire in those slate-blue eyes. As always, there was a watchful waiting, an electric awareness that measured her every reaction. She'd never been involved with a man capable of exhibiting such restraint and self-control. And yet, even though he lived behind walls, the man had willingly stepped between her and a speeding emotional bullet.

The memory snagged at her heart, because it was something Thomas had never attempted to do. Instead, when his success had been threatened, he'd dumped her via the *Bricklin Daily Sentinel*. No warning. No phone call. Just her in her PJs, with a cup of coffee on a beautiful Sunday morning, and an article about what was next for the candidate running for California State Senate. Apparently her boyfriend's backup plan had been to feed her to the wolves—despite his vow to stick by her through the scandal.

And then, of course, there was her father's emotional desertion...

The painful memories robbed her of her breath even as the irony tightened her lips into a thin smile. How lame did it make her that she was so grateful that someone had finally stood up for her? Someone who wasn't even family or involved with her in a relationship. No, it was the guy she'd challenged to a very public duel.

What would it be like to make love to Hunter? She'd had her fair share of boyfriends, and was no stranger to sexual attraction, but she'd always been a little disappointed by how quickly it faded. How bored she became. Of course she'd never known anyone quite like the sexy, intense, white-hat-wearing Hunter Philips.

Don't do it, Carly. Don't do it! It's only lust.

But it wasn't really. It was much more complicated than that. And still, despite the fact she shouldn't, a part of her had to finish what she'd started.

Gathering her courage, she crossed to the gym bag, fished out some quarters and headed for the machine, not stopping to think about her plan any further. Fingers clumsy with desire—and a generous dose of nerves—she struggled with the mechanism but couldn't get the knob to twist. She smacked it in frustration.

Okay, so maybe the lust and nerves were a little stronger than usual.

"Let me." A wet hand rested on her left hip as an arm reached around her on the right, and a sensual longing swept through her so strong her knees almost gave way. Her mind froze, chanting out the change in circumstances.

Hunter. Naked. An embrace, of sorts, from behind. From Hunter.

Naked.

Breath fanning her temple, a damp heat emanating from his body, he turned the knob, his movements calm, collected. A condom dropped into the tray with a promising thunk. Carly turned her back to the wall beside the dispenser, examining his naked body. It was still a glorious sight, made much more devastating by his proximity. The lean, well-muscled chest peppered with dark hair. The taut abdomen and the long, powerful thighs. The straining erection.

Even now he seemed so sure of himself. So cool. Deliberate.

His eyes bored into hers. "Will we need more than one?"

With her body's current state of arousal she might not survive the first round. But there was no need to let him know how he affected her. Mouth dry, fingers shaky, she lifted her blouse over her head and tossed it aside. "It all hinges on your stamina."

He nodded at the machine and its display of graphic diagrams. "I choose the second go around."

Heart galloping nervously, she held his gaze as she removed her bra. "Just as long as it's not number five."

He inserted a second quarter into the machine. Eyes on hers, his gaze lit with a mix of humor, bone-melting desire and blatant challenge, he slowly twisted the knob. He *had* to know every crank was bringing her closer to the edge. "How about a modified version?" he said.

The mechanism caught, and a second thunk occurred.

Carly's insides twisted. Their relentless game of cat and mouse was leaving her coiled tight, never knowing which way was up. Or who had the upper hand. If either of them did.

"What if your sparring partner walks in on us?" she said.

His enigmatic smile returned as he pressed her against the wall. The tile was cold against her already over-heated skin. "Let's just hope he doesn't," he murmured as he lowered his head.

The moment his lips touched hers Carly responded eagerly. He pressed her mouth open, his tongue taking hers. The soul-drugging kiss pushed what little reason she had aside as his hands made quick work of her jeans and her panties, pushing them to the floor. Hunter sought the warm flesh between her legs, teasing her until she trembled, slick against his fingers. Her body's ready response was so quick it was almost embarrassing.

It's only lust, Carly.

Carly pulled her mouth a fraction from his, surprised her

voice was so unsteady. "I thought I was supposed to be seducing you."

His mouth moved to her neck, his fingers making her body
sing, and he said, "You'll get your turn."

Hunter pressed well-placed, open-mouthed kisses on her
shoulder, tasting her on his way to her breast. Her skin tin-
gled in the wake.

Struggling to get the words out, she said, "Just remember—" His lips landed on a puckered tip, searing her nerves,
and she arched against him. She closed her eyes and went on.
"You promised two rounds."

One hand on her hip, the other between her legs, he drove
her insane, his mouth traveling down her abdomen with intent. His words whispered across her belly. "When did I do
that?"

"You bought a second condom." Her voice was weak.
"That's an implied promise, isn't it?"

"Guess we'll find out."

She hoped they would, but she was too immersed in mind-
bending pleasure to tell him.

Fire licked her veins, incinerating her every thought as his
mouth crossed her hip on the way to her inner thigh. Carly
instinctively spread her legs a little more, a welcoming gesture, and Hunter took full advantage of the invitation, replac-
ing the teasing fingers with his mouth.

Her heart imploded, sensual forces gripping her hard.
With a sharp hiss, Carly dropped her head back. His lips,
teeth and tongue worked their spell on her body. So focused.
His movements deliberate. Skilled. Strategically planned for
maximum pleasure. Until Carly was shaking, the nape of her
neck damp with sweat.

As his lips drove her closer to the sun, Hunter slid his
hands up her belly to cup her breasts. His thumbs circled
the tips, and solar touchdown became a near certainty. Back

pressed against the cool tile, her body suffused with heat, Carly gripped his shoulders, her thighs trembling. Eyes closed, she gasped for breath. Flames of desire climbed higher, blinding her with white-hot light. Until Carly's body finally launched fully into the inferno. The orgasm consumed her, fanning out in a fireball of pleasure, and she called out Hunter's name.

As her cry echoed off the tile, Hunter stood and took in Carly's flushed face. Her eyes were closed, hair damp at her temples. The quiet was broken by the harsh sounds coming from Carly's throat, her chest heaving as she struggled to catch her breath.

The moment she'd entered the shower room, deep down he'd known where it would lead, despite his attempts to drive her away. And with the risk she posed to the peace he'd achieved with his past, thwarting her attempt to run the show had seemed necessary, her bold moves, her gutsy nature captivating him like no other.

Which was why pushing her up against the wall and taking charge had been so important.

Eyes still closed, her voice steady despite the breathless quality, Carly said, "Does that count as a round?"

"I was just getting you warmed up."

"Well done, you," she said softly. She lifted her lids, her gaze meeting his. "Now..." she slid her arms around his neck, her eyes dark with desire "...take me to the bench."

Hunter's heart thumped hard. Take-charge Carly was back, and need coiled tightly in his groin, choking off any hope of refusing her anything. Blocking all thoughts of the past. The beautifully outrageous, never-backs-down woman created fires within him he might never be able to extinguish.

The surge of alarm he felt at the thought wasn't enough

to change his mind, but it made his voice harsh. "Grab both condoms," he said, and she complied.

Hunter lifted her, and she wrapped her legs around his waist. As he carried her across the room the head of his shaft nudged the wet warmth between her legs, teasing him with its proximity. Taunting him with its readiness. Everything about her tested his restraint. She arched against him, pressing him closer, clearly wanting him inside. He straddled the wooden bench, one foot on either side, and sat on his towel with Carly on his lap, her legs draped around him. Gritting his teeth, fighting the need to thrust deep, he began to lean her back.

But was stopped by her hand on his chest.

Carly's voice was low, determined. "My turn. My choice." Gaze locked with his, she said, "So lie down, Mystery Man." His muscles tensed, but he let her press him back, coming to a stop when his elbows rested on the bench. Refusing to concede any more ground. She tipped her head seductively. "I want to see how long it takes for you to come unglued."

Hunter's lungs constricted as pleasure, anticipation and uneasiness wrapped around his chest, their position on the bench bringing reality home. Outside the frequency and duration of his relationships he hadn't noticed the subtle shift in his sexual life since he'd been played, like his tendency to gravitate toward women who were fairly passive.

Until right now, until Carly, he hadn't realized just how much he'd lost with his choices.

Heart pumping, agitated, Hunter stared up at her amber eyes. Her glossy brown hair fanned across her breasts, and he was incredibly turned on not only by her dominant posture as she straddled his lap but also by her aggressive moves. Despite his troubled thoughts, desire was the clear winner, made obvious by the fact he was so hot he was ready to burst. It all got worse when she cupped his face, lowered her head, and kissed him with a potency that seared him from the inside out, slanting her mouth across his.

Lips and tongues engaged in a duel, she dragged her nails down his chest, scraping the flat nipples, and a groan escaped him. In response, Carly gently began to move her hips, rubbing her slick center along his hard length. Sweat beaded at his temples as he fought the urge to take over. The sensual moment went on, lingering, driving him mad, until she tore her mouth away, sat up and opened a foil packet. When she grasped his erection his blood sang, and his every cell urged her to hurry as she rolled the condom on. With the look of a woman who knew what she wanted, she positioned herself over him and he arched up to meet her, going deep.

"Hunter," Carly groaned, her eyes flaring wide with shock and delight. And then her lids fluttered closed, as if the strength of her desire surprised her as much as his pleasure at her boldness did him.

But that hardly seemed possible.

She splayed her hands on his chest and began to rock her hips, nails digging into his flesh as she arched her back, angling to absorb more of him. He met her thrust for thrust. Eyes closed, cheeks flushed, her mouth parted, she—without hesitation or apology—slowly drove him higher. Pushed him further. Giving him what he craved. All the fire and sultry passion that had turned his head from day one was present in her movements.

Backing him closer to a line he didn't want to cross.

Rocking his hips in time with hers, bench hard against his elbows, he clenched his fists, slipping further under her spell with every painfully pleasurable moment. Her soft body, her citrusy scent and her relentless, no-holds-barred attitude gained more ground, stretching his reserve. Dragging him closer to the edge.

As if she sensed his waning restraint, Carly tunneled her

fingers into his hair and brought her mouth back down, devouring him. Desire shot through his veins, carrying the compelling need to the far reaches of his body. Drowning in the intensely disturbing feeling, he knew he should take over to preserve his sanity. The fact that he couldn't, *wouldn't*, made him angry with himself. Even as she consumed him, increasing the pace. Her mouth and hips greedy. Demanding he give up everything.

Carly dropped her hands to his buttocks and shifted, taking him deeper between her legs.

And he lost a little more of his hard-won control.

Carly lifted her lips a fraction, her gaze burning into his as she whispered wicked words that feathered across his mouth, her voice mesmerizing as she slowly pushed him back until he lay flat on the bench. She leaned over him, relentless as she made love to him from above. Her sweet smell, her softness and her seductive ways were threatening to undo him. His abdomen tensed. His sweat-slicked skin was damp against the wood bench as he fought the exquisite sensation of being immersed. Surrounded. Holding on by a thread.

Carly's moans grew more frequent. More urgent. And Hunter slid deeper, losing more of himself with every passing moment as Carly drew him closer to the flame. And then Carly cried out and her nails dug deep into his skin.

Like a bolt of lightning his control cracked, incinerating him in a blinding flash even as his mind went blank, engulfed by the terrible pleasure. He arched his neck and wrapped his arms around her waist, pumping his hips wildly. Bucking hard. His need desperate and dangerous. Almost destructive. With a harsh groan, Hunter clutched Carly closer as his muscles burned, tensed and coiled ever tighter. And when the pressure became so fierce he thought it would destroy him it snapped, releasing him with a force that shot him into oblivion.

CHAPTER SEVEN

"CARLY."

The lilting female voice cut through the murmur of guests in formal wear in the posh, expansive living room of William Wolfe's home. From the doorway leading to the back corridor—her only means of an easy escape—Carly spied the wife of the CFO of Wolfe Broadcasting approaching. Though she was pushing seventy, through the magic of expensive surgery Elaine Bennett's face had a mask-like look that defied designation.

For a moment Carly was a teensy bit jealous, because she felt as if she'd aged ten years in the week since she'd last seen Hunter, walking away from her at the gym.

Elaine Bennett's beaded black evening dress glittered in the light as she approached. "Your father must be so happy you're here."

Ignoring the urge to contradict her, Carly submitted to an air kiss from the woman. "Mrs. Bennett, you look lovely."

The woman eyed her with the critical affection of one who had known Carly since she was five, and when the lady lifted a perfectly plucked brow Carly knew it would be followed by a carefully targeted reproof. "Since you moved back to Miami we hardly see you. Your father isn't getting any younger, you know," Mrs. Bennett said, almost as if aging was a sin. "You shouldn't be such a stranger, Carly."

millsandboon.co.uk

Get an **EXCLUSIVE 15% OFF ORDERS**

when you order online today!

Simply enter the code **15JUN12** as you checkout and the discount will automatically be applied to your order. **BUT HURRY**, this offer ends on 30th June 2012.

All of the latest titles are available 1 MONTH AHEAD of the shops, **PLUS:**

- **Titles available in paperback and eBook**
- **Huge savings** on titles you may have missed
- **Try before you buy** with Browse the Book

Shop now at **millsandboon.co.uk**

JUN12

Nerves stretched tight, Carly murmured a noncommittal response and took a fortifying sip of her champagne as she watched Mrs. Bennett return to the other guests, dreading the thought of a run-in with her father. Their relationship had always been tenuous, at best, but since the Thomas Weaver Affair it had been as fragile as Abby's good humor.

She wouldn't have accepted her father's invitation—except *not* coming would suggest she was too ashamed to show. Or, worse, paint her as petulant. The elegant party was in honor of Brian O'Connor, not her—God forbid her father should ever celebrate his daughter. No, it was Brian O'Connor who had delivered a surge in ratings with the shocking history behind Hunter Philips's app—a scoop that had been avidly sought by others. The host had even secured a third show, which was now being hyped in the media as guaranteed to be a monumental success. And there was nothing William Wolfe admired more than success.

Hence his strained relationship with his disappointing failure of a daughter.

Carly gripped her champagne flute, refusing to let old emotions from her teenage years drag her down. She'd make her appearance, hold her head high and prove to her father she wasn't ashamed of her life, avoiding any one-on-one conversations. Because, after six sketchy nights of sleep, unable to keep her mind off of making love to Hunter, she didn't have the energy for a confrontation tonight.

She scanned the growing crowd, spying Brian O'Connor schmoozing with her father, and tension snaked between her shoulders. She longed for the appearance of a few naked actors, Harley-riders or drag queens—anything to liven up the party and get her mind off her current train of thought.

And then, as if the powers that be had heard her wish, Hunter entered the room, wearing a beautiful tuxedo. Her heart did a double take and her mind slipped back to the moment her world had collided with a new reality...

Stunned, Carly had clung to Hunter after they'd made love, pulse pounding, chest heaving. She wasn't quite sure what had happened, only that her body had been taken to heights that normally would require rocket fuel—and her ability to recover from the event had been greatly impaired by the knowledge of how aggressive she'd been. She'd wanted him, and had no regrets, but she'd all but hunted him down and backed him into a corner. So it had been hard to maintain that easy-breezy attitude when it was over. Especially when Hunter had retreated behind his wall.

He'd been coolly polite but decidedly detached as they'd spent an awkward few minutes getting dressed, the silence in the locker room consuming every available oxygen molecule. Carly had considered asking why he'd bothered obtaining a second condom, but her chance had ended when Hunter, ever the protector, had escorted her to her car and calmly walked away without a backward glance.

But right now he was headed in her direction.

Shoulder propped against the doorjamb, she gripped her clutch purse, smoothing a damp palm down the silk of her crimson spaghetti-strap dress. A dress that showed off way more leg than it should. At least she was appropriately attired.

Pushing aside the nerves, she said, "Mr. Philips—"

"Hunter."

His demeanor was *über*-cool, untouched, his gaze as sharply alert as ever—a far cry from the man who'd briefly come unhinged in her arms. He eyed her over his glass as he sipped his champagne, the absurdity of her use of his last name radiating from his gaze.

"Nice house," he said, nodding at the lavishly furnished living room, the moonless night obscuring its view of the Atlantic.

"Don't let it fool you." Her gaze swept across the imported tile and Brazilian cherrywood walls that gave off a warm, welcoming glow, carefully designed by an interior decorator with the blessing of her father. "It was decorated for effect," she went on dryly. "To create the illusion of warmth and comfort."

They spent a few tension-filled seconds staring at one another, until Hunter's gaze roamed down her body, lingering briefly on her legs, and a surge of remembered desire suffused her in heat. By the collected look on his face she knew it was a deliberate act.

His hint of a smile didn't quite reach his eyes. "Any number of things can be faked in this day and age."

His tone set her on edge, and she gripped the champagne flute hard. "For example?"

His eyes scanned the crowd of people and paused on Mrs. Bennett. "Youth."

Despite her amusement, the strained air prevented a smile. "Caring?" she said, forcing herself to hold his gaze. "Compassion?"

His words came out deceptively soft, his focus intense. "Or an orgasm."

The statement hit hard, leaving a trail of popping electrical energy as it settled deeper in her brain. She tried to decide which was worse: him thinking she was a reckless fool or that her participation had all been an act.

Stunned, she stared at him. What had started as a game that day in the alley had led to something that now felt deadly serious—a grave threat to her sanity, her peace of mind and her heart. And the tightrope of emotional peril she was crossing with Hunter was one she'd never attempted before. Toss in an intensely hot sexual experience and—well, a girl was bound to feel a little unnerved. Because there was nothing more beautiful than Hunter Philips coming unglued. Of course, getting him there had taken a Herculean effort. He'd resisted her to the bitter end. And as soon as it was over the wall had returned. So what did that say about his opinion of her?

Her stomach twisted, and she fought the urge to retreat down the hall to safety.

Keep it light, Carly. Keep it easy.

She cleared her throat, rallying her mojo. "I can't begin to tell you how crushed I'll be if you confess you faked your way through Sunday night."

The words briefly cut through the tension, easing the intensity in Hunter's eyes a touch. "That's where women hold a distinct advantage over men."

"Since that often isn't the case, I'll take it where I can."

His gaze dropped to her legs, his brow creased in humor. "I'm quite sure you will."

Struggling for her usual self-assurance, she leaned her back against the doorjamb. "You're just jealous I had visual confirmation you were very turned on." She sent him the best charming smile she could, given the circumstances. "Helped, of course, by the fact that you leave evidence behind when you fire off your…bullets."

He smiled. "You're not jealous of my weapon, are you?"

"No gun-envy here." She took a step closer and got a whiff of his cologne, bringing sensual memories of the locker room, and her tone turned huskier than she'd planned. "But you should teach me how to shoot yours."

His body grew still and heat flared in his eyes. His tone matched his gaze. "That could be arranged." His voice lowered to a rumble that was a mix of potent desire and distrust. "Would you approach that with pretend enthusiasm? Or would it be real?"

He clearly wasn't comfortable with her motivation in the locker room. But the truth was too painful, cut too close to her heart, to share. What was she supposed to say? That she'd never had anyone come to her rescue before? That she'd been the damsel in distress in the past, but no knight in shining armor had ever risked anything to ride to her defense? Her profound appreciation of his gesture of protection was so enormous it was pathetic. Almost needy.

And she was a confident woman. She shouldn't have been so desperate to conquer this man's reserve. It wasn't as if it proved he cared about her in any way. Or felt she was worthy of his on-air sacrifice…

Her breath hitched, but she pushed away the thought and steadily met his gaze. "Are you questioning the integrity of my responses?"

"Maybe."

She placed a hand on her hip. "Were my moans not authentic enough?"

"The moans seemed genuine."

"Were my groans lacking in honesty?"

"Your groans sounded sincere." He hesitated, and his tone grew heavy with meaning. "It was the shout at the end that I questioned."

The shout had been real, all right. She refused to look away. "I'm crushed you're second-guessing my enthusiasm."

His eyes held hers as the moments ticked by. When he spoke, there was suspicion and frustration in his tone. "I have no doubt your enthusiasm for your *job* is real."

Devastated by the insinuation, Carly could almost hear the creaking sound as his statement strained under the weighty load of meaning.

Outside of Thomas she'd never been involved with a man who'd hurt her when he'd walked away, as they all invariably did. Yet here she was, with a guy she wasn't even dating, wounded by his ability to take her in an explosion of hunger, calmly walk away, and with his next breath accuse her of dishonesty. Which meant he had a power over her no man had had ever before. Damn. The smile on her face grew tight, but she pushed back the need to pop the cork on her anger.

Don't go there. Don't let the emotion get the best of you.

But her aggravation was evident in her hardened tone. "I wonder if your doubt is a reflection of my past—" she moved closer, ignoring his wonderful scent and the hard physique encased in an elegant tuxedo "—or yours."

His gaze didn't waver, but a muscle in Hunter's cheek twitched. Four pounding heartbeats later he went on. "Before this conversation continues, I think a break is in order. I'll get us more champagne," he said as he took her empty glass, the heat smoldering in his eyes searing her to the bone, "but I'll be back."

She watched him head toward the bar and let out a breath, unaware she'd been holding it. But before she could relax another masculine voice spoke from behind.

"Hello, kitten."

At the sound of her childhood nickname her heart took an abrupt turn in her chest, speeding south. She briefly closed her eyes, preparing to face the man who doubted her more than most.

As Carly braced to face her father her stomach bunched into a knot. She was dreading his simmering judgment about her career, her life choices—and her *mistake*. She was used to the disapproving tone in his every comment. No matter how hard she tried, her efforts had never been good enough. But she was an adult now. She didn't need his praise. And she sure wouldn't beg him for approval.

Her moody, miserable, misunderstood teen years had been rough, and she'd constantly butted heads with her father. Unfortunately traces of that rebellious adolescent were reappearing more and more of late in his presence. She didn't like herself much when he was around. Which was the main reason she'd avoided him for the last six months.

Keep your cool, Carly. Keep it easy. And, whatever you do, don't let him see you cry.

Turning on her heel, she plastered a smile on her face. "Hello, Dad."

His hair now more gray than black, he was a striking figure of a man in his sixties. Tall. Fit. With his sharp features, he was imposing via the sheer volume of his eyebrows alone. And twenty-five years as head of a mega news corporation had honed his hard stare to a cutting edge.

"I assumed you wouldn't come," he said.

Good to see you too, Dad. I'm fine, thanks. How have you been?

She pushed aside the disappointment at his less than welcoming greeting. She knew better, and she really had to stop hoping for more. "Is that the only reason I was included on the guestlist?" she asked.

The muscles around his eyes tightened a touch. "If I didn't want you here I wouldn't have invited you."

Well," she said, trying to keep it light, "I suppose it would have looked bad if you'd invited everyone from the show except your own daughter."

His eyes grew wary and he frowned at her too-short dress, creating a flush of guilt-tinged resentment. Okay, so the hem length was a bit much. But she didn't need any more proof that he disapproved. Of course her father must have felt a sarcastic comment was in order.

"You've outdone even yourself tonight," he said. "Who's the poor guy this time?"

Her stomach balled tighter as she blinked back the pain. "I didn't bring a date." She tipped her head. "Disappointed?"

Her father's mouth went flat. "Can't say I'm eager to meet the latest good-for-nothing."

"Good-for-nothing?"

"Face it, Carly," he said, scanning the room before turning his gaze back to hers. "You should give your choice of men more thought before you hook up with them—or whatever you young folks call it these days."

Inhaling a calming breath, Carly straightened her shoulders, forcing an even tone. "Every guy I've *dated*," she said, mustering her patience, "has been a decent man."

"Every one of them has lacked ambition."

"I don't choose my dates based on the man's ambition for his job and his fat bank account." As a matter of fact, those attributes usually sent her screaming in the other direction. Hunter Philips was the single exception—for all the good it did her.

The displeasure in her father's eyes tunneled the hole deeper in her heart. "You set your standards too low, kitten."

"Maybe yours are set too high?" she countered.

The pause in the conversation was loaded as they regarded each other warily, and she wondered—*again*—why she'd bothered to come.

When her father went on, this time his tone was full of bewildered frustration. "The worst part is I don't think you care about your boyfriends that much. Instead you try on one fellow after another, and then wonder why they treat you so poorly in the end."

The words landed too close for comfort. "Is that what this party is really about?" Carly asked. "An excuse to get me here and harass me about my love-life?"

"It's a sad day when I have to throw a party just to see my own daughter." He let out the same long-suffering, resigned sigh he always did. The one that made her feel awful. "But as for your love-life," he went on, "you're an adult. Who you choose to run around with is your business."

"That's never stopped you from sharing your opinion."

"I'm more concerned about your professional choices."

Her heart withered a fraction as humiliation and shame came roaring back, and her patience slipped further from her grasp. "Come on, Dad. It's me. No need to sugar-coat your words." She stepped closer. "Why don't you just say you're worried I'll screw up again? Repeat past mistakes?" The frown on her father's face wasn't an answer, but it was all the response that Carly needed. "Well, there *is* good news. If I do muck it up a second time, at least it won't be on one of your newspapers. So you don't have to worry about that precious bottom line of yours."

Getting fired was her fault, not her dad's. But her sharp stab of doubt about his role in the debacle still cut deep.

She stared at her father, and for once the truth spilled out, free of sarcasm. "It's been three years, and I still can't decide if you were the one who ordered my dismissal or not."

Her dad's face flushed red, and he stepped closer. "Damn it, Carly," he said, the affectionate nickname long gone. "Your boss made that decision. Were you truly so naive as to think there wouldn't be repercussions?" He narrowed his eyes in disbelief, as if he still couldn't fathom how she could have been so stupid. "Just like you were naive enough to believe Thomas Weaver wasn't using you?"

"He *wasn't* using me. We didn't start dating until three months after my story ran." She lifted her chin, batting back the overwhelming emotion. "However I *was* naive enough to believe that the people who cared about me would stick around when things got ugly. But when the going got tough he turned his back on me to save himself. Just like you."

"What did you expect me to do, Carly?" he said. "Make excuses about my daughter's lack of judgment? Show a preference for my own flesh and blood? I run a tight ship, and business has to come first." His face shifted from anger and frustration—which she could handle—to the worst expression of all…disappointment. "I don't understand how you could have made such a rookie mistake."

She swallowed against a tight throat, her words thick. "I have a heart, Dad."

"Whether you choose to believe it or not, I do too."

"But I can't turn it on and off like you."

"As I've said…" His scowl grew deeper. "I couldn't step in on your behalf."

The pressure of budding tears burned her lids, and she tightened her grip on her purse. "Don't you get it, Daddy?" The name slipped out before she knew what she was saying. "I didn't *want* you to step in on my behalf," she said. She'd waited forever to hear her father say he believed in her. And here she was, three years later, still waiting in vain. "You have no faith in me at all, do you? I would *never* have asked you to show me that kind of favor." She fought to control the ferocious hurt. "But you didn't even trust me enough to give me the option of turning it down."

Though her dad's face broiled with anger, when Hunter appeared at her side with the champagne her father nodded in his direction and said, "Clearly *you're* too smart to fall prey to my daughter's charms."

Her heart convulsed, and Carly wasn't sure which was worse—the shame or the pain. She tried to respond, but her reply died when Hunter smoothly stepped closer to her side. A silent promise of protection.

His frigid, steel-like gaze focused on her father and he voiced an icy word of warning. "Careful."

But this was one encounter Hunter couldn't save her from. Wrestling with the need to cry, scream and lash out with her words, Carly blinked back the roiling anger. If she didn't leave now she'd make a fool of herself. After a last glance at her father's fuming face, she pivoted on her heel and headed out of the living room, leaving the murmur of happy chatter behind.

CHAPTER EIGHT

As William Wolfe stomped off, Hunter watched Carly head down the hallway and wrestled with the intense urge to follow her, resisting the impulse. Despite the danger she posed, he'd shown up tonight because he couldn't seem to deny himself the pleasure of Carly Wolfe's company.

After they'd made love, his body completely spent, he'd realized the liberating release had been like none he'd experienced before. And he'd wanted her again. The moment the craving had hit he'd remembered exactly why she'd followed him into the shower room. Plagued by the disturbing thought she was using him, he'd had to bolt or risk losing himself in her a second time. And when he'd spied her sinfully sexy dress tonight, need had smashed him head-on. Angry at himself for being so susceptible, he'd provoked her. Insulted her…just like her father.

Regret churned in his gut. After the scene he'd just witnessed, he had a better understanding of the complex woman so full of softly rounded corners and sharp edges. Brashly forward, yet remarkably vulnerable. Driven at her job, yet oddly innocent at the same time. Hunter still wasn't entirely clear which side of the Carly equation *he* fell on—or, in the end, which side she would choose—but he was now convinced she was innocent of every accusation the press had thrown at her three years ago.

Fingers gripping the champagne flutes, he watched her turn into a room at the end of the hall feeling torn, grappling with the need not to be played for a fool again. But at least when he'd suffered his parents had supported him. Booker had stuck by him. But Carly...

When Carly had made her so-called mistake she'd been abandoned by the two people that had mattered most. The knowledge took a chink from his heart and burned in ways it shouldn't.

Jaw clenched, decision made, he left the party behind and strode down the long corridor, stopping in the open doorway at the end. Color high on her cheeks, mouth set, Carly paced the length of a masculine office done in forest-green, a bordering-on-indecent length of silky leg swishing back and forth beneath her red dress.

He hesitated, and debated changing his mind. Instead he said, "You want to tell me what just happened?"

She never broke her stride, and her tone matched the fury in her pace. "I want you to leave."

He was used to her charm-and-slash smile, the targeted sarcastic comments and the intentional flirting, but he'd never seen her so blatantly angry before. Not even when he'd insulted her.

Champagne in hand, he slowly entered the room. "I think you should talk about it."

"No," she bit out, looking close to either blowing her top or bursting into tears.

He set the glasses on a massive walnut desk. "You might feel better if you cried."

"No." Mid-stride, she heaved her purse onto the leather office chair. In a woman who normally brimmed with self-confidence the stark emotion, the seething vulnerability on her face, was hard to watch. "I promised myself I wouldn't cry about it again. Especially not *here*."

His heart twisted, but he ignored it. "Why not here?"

She reached the far wall and turned, heading back in his direction. "Right after the Weaver story blew up in my face and I got fired I came home, looking for support." Still pacing, she pointed in the direction of the desk, eyes burning with emotion. "And the moment I got back he sat me in this office and lectured me on a reporter's duty and the main goal of a paper…to make money. He went on and on about the importance of the financial bottom line." Her eyes looked suspiciously bright, but no tears welled. "He didn't give a *damn* how I felt."

It was the restraint that almost did him in.

She passed him, her scent trailing in her wake.

"Nothing I do is ever good enough. I've avoided him for six months." She fisted her hands. "Six *months*. And in less than two minutes he's making cracks about my love-life."

He watched her retrace her path across the room. "Has your relationship with your father always been difficult?"

"No," she said. "In some ways that would make it easier. Then I could just walk away. Instead I moved back to Miami." Her lips pressed in a thin line. "And like a moron I hang around, remembering how it used to be when I was younger…"

It was a dilemma he understood well. Lately he'd been spending a lot of time dealing with the past himself. He let out a long, slow breath. "It's hard to cut the good memories loose just to free yourself from the bad."

She stopped in the middle of the room and her gaze met his. "Exactly."

They studied one another for a moment. Several heartbeats passed and Hunter felt the pull, much as he had in the locker room. But this time it was so much more than sexual. Uncomfortable, he crossed his arms. "When did you two start having trouble?"

A shadow briefly flashed across her face, and she looked a little lost standing in the center of the room. "My mom died when I was a baby, so Dad's the only family I have. Things got rough when I hit my teens," she said, threading less than steady fingers through her hair. "Since then all he's done is berate me over every decision I make, all the way down to the clothes I choose to wear. Pretty soon, I just gave up." Her mouth twisted grimly, and she smoothed her hand down the silk covering her thighs. "I wore this dress tonight because I knew it would piss my father off." After a self-derisive scoff, she shook her head and turned to stare desolately out a night-blackened window. When she spoke it was almost as if to herself. "I don't know why I continue to antagonize him."

He knew. "Strike first before you get knocked out. It's a protective habit." He had a few of those himself.

She looked at him as if the idea was new to her. "Yeah," she said. "He's been known to throw a few fast punches. He once accused me of treating boyfriends like shoes from the sale rack." He lifted a brow in question, and she went on. "Tried on, adored for a few months, and then relegated to the back of the closet."

He leaned his shoulder against the wood-paneled wall. "Have there been a lot of men?"

"More than a few. Less than too many." She stared at him a moment before hiking her chin a touch. "Are you judging me?"

"No," he said truthfully. "It's not my place to judge. Why do these relationships end?"

"My fault, probably." With a self-conscious shrug, she sent him a small smile of defeat. "I get bored, and I suspect the guys can sense it."

Curious, he pushed off the wall and moved closer to Carly. "And what does the turnover rate provide you with?"

She let out a bark of laughter, as if the question was absurd. When he didn't return the humor she seemed to give the question some thought. "Mostly just a lot of embarrassing break-ups." She cocked her head. "Did you know there's a singing telegram service in town that specializes in break-up messages? I'm probably the only recipient in Miami whose address they know by heart." He bit back the smile as she went on dryly. "So the only thing the turnover rate provides me with is a lot of jokes in the office at my expense."

"And maybe another method of making your father angry?"

Her scowl was instantaneous. "No," she said, and then her expression softened to include a bit of uncertainty. "Maybe." She bit her lower lip, and then doubt replaced the frown completely. "I don't know," she said slowly, as if contemplating the possibility.

He stepped closer, looking down at her face. "Or maybe you don't want anyone around long enough to use you again. Like the senator did."

Denial surged, and her tone was adamant. "Thomas did *not* use me."

He studied her for a bit, wondering who she was trying to convince. Him...or herself.

"Are you sure?" He paused long enough to get her full attention. To hammer his point home. "That's hard to believe, seeing how when you finally became a hindrance instead of an asset he cut you loose."

"My story was already out. How was I an ass—?"

"With Wolfe Broadcasting in his pocket, winning elections would be a lot easier."

Carly closed her eyes, looking as if she'd been struck, and Hunter wanted to kick himself for being so blunt.

"Jeez." She paused, and then inhaled deeply as if to steady herself. "You're hell on a girl's ego, you know," she said softly. "I don't know what to believe anymore." She lifted her lids, and her gaze held an aching vulnerability that killed him. "All I know is…"

It seemed there was plenty she didn't *want* to know. "What?" he said quietly.

She scanned his gaze and her amber eyes lost a little of the gold as the brown intensified, growing darker. "All I know is that I want you again."

Heat and need socked him in the gut, setting off a sensual storm that promised to sweep away his resolve. This wasn't the reason he'd followed her here, but there was no flirtatious tone. No coy looks. No sassy challenge in her eyes. Just an open honesty that was clearly a cover for a painful defenselessness that made her scent, her soft skin and the desire in her eyes all the more difficult to resist.

His heart was pulling double duty, trying to keep the blood supporting his brain even as it drained to his groin. Outwardly he might appear calm, but Carly had to feel the earth quaking from the hammering in his chest. "Why?"

"Because you make me feel like nobody else ever has."

As he scrutinized her face, looking for the truth, he realized that making love to him in her father's house would be the perfect retribution for her.

Despite the need to pace, the restless urge to move, instead he said, "I should leave."

"Please stay."

His body now fully on board for anything she had planned, despite the fact his brain thought it a bad idea, he said, "It isn't fair, asking me while you're wearing that dress." His words were throatier than he would have liked. "I don't even think it's legal."

She tipped her head in that sexy way that slayed him. "Will you arrest me if it isn't?"

"I probably should," he muttered. He held her gaze, fiercely aroused and intensely troubled. Was he just another way for

Carly to get back at her father? Or an effective method for burying all those self-doubts?

For a brief moment he wondered if she wanted something more from him.

And what if she did?

Doubt battled desire, twisting his heart into impossible shapes, and he muttered his next thought out loud. "What other weapons do you have up your non-existent sleeves?"

She blinked several times and after a brief deliberation lifted her arms, placing her hands on her head in mock surrender. A position of submission. As if yielding all power to Hunter. "You can frisk me and look for more if you want," she said.

She steadily met his gaze...and he knew she was waiting for him to make his choice.

Gathering her courage, Carly waited, hating how much this man destroyed her usual confidence. He was hot, intriguing and dangerous, even when coming to her defense. And he never failed to step up on her behalf when it mattered most. She'd never fallen for a man before, and a part of her had always wondered why. With Hunter, she feared she was already more than halfway there...

Her heart skipped a beat and her stomach settled lower.

It's only lust, Carly.

She felt bare, exposed and defenseless as the seconds crawled by while he studied her, as if trying to decide what to do. Although the fire and focus in his eyes communicated he wanted her, it was obvious he questioned her motives.

But the unadorned truth was too hard to share: no matter how hard she worked, or how happy she tried to be, the sadness over her fractured relationship with her father made peace of mind impossible. Hunter's square-cut jaw, sensual lips and broad shoulders—and, more importantly, his protector mode she found so attractive—threatened to consume her as well. And she was desperate for the latter to win. Even if it was only for another sensually mind-boggling moment. It wasn't a difficult choice, really. Who wouldn't choose feel-good promise over dark disappointment?

Hope over despair?

Hands on her head, she stared at him, dying to know if he was as good as she remembered. Maybe she'd just been pathetically grateful for his on-air act of gallantry, sacrificing himself for her? Maybe it had been how hard he'd fought her in the locker room, and how utterly beautiful he'd been when he'd taken the fall? Or maybe she was simply tired of guys so laid-back they were just one step above dead?

"Frisk you?" he mused as he finally closed the last bit of distance between them, his rumbling voice shimmying down her spine. "I probably should." Meeting her gaze, he laid his hands on her wrists, skimming his way down her bare arms. The skin-on-skin feel left goosebumps in their wake. "Just to be safe." He smoothed his palms down her sides, his thumbs brushing the outer edges of her breasts in tantalizing promise before slowing to a crawl at her hips.

His gaze burned into hers, the warm hands scalding her through thin silk. "What are you wearing underneath?" he said.

"A thong."

His eyes turned darker as he slowly crouched. "Anything else?" he said, smoothing his sizzling hands down her legs.

Anticipation reached critical levels, and her palms grew hot against her head. "Nothing."

He looked up at her from his squatting position, hands on her shins. "That means there aren't many hiding places under this dress."

Her heart pounded at the memories of the last time he'd knelt in front of her. "It depends on how thorough you are."

The mysterious smile was instantaneous. He smoothed his hands up over her knees, higher along her thighs, and stroked the sensitive nub between her legs. Awash in pleasure, heart battering her chest, Carly maintained his gaze even as her thong grew wet.

"I'm motivated to be very thorough," he murmured.

He lingered a moment, eyes so dark it was hard to remember them ever being cold. Her body was so hot and damp it was hard to be much more than a mass of needy nerve endings.

"Because you're a G-man following procedure?" she said, her voice breathless.

"Why else?" He stood, his hands smoothing up her belly, between her breasts, out and around both, before finally cupping the curves. "Technically I should check your back too." His thumbs skimmed her now taut nipples and pleasure surged, her body melting more. She fought to focus as he said, "But it's occurred to me you don't need any armaments beyond this."

His mouth claimed hers and she kissed him back with all the pent-up, conflicting emotions in her chest. Desire for Hunter, and fear of giving him too much power over her. Hunter simply took what he wanted, demanding everything, and Carly could do little more than comply.

Heat infused her every cell as his hands slid under her dress to clasp her buttocks, pulling her firmly against his hard length. She arched against him in agreement, their mouths engaged in a primal duel even as his thumbs smoothed soothing circles low on her back.

"We need to lock the door," she murmured between rough kisses.

"We need a condom," he said against her mouth.

"The second one from the dispenser is in my purse."

At her words, he pulled his head back, eyes still fiery with need, his brow creased in surprise. She had grabbed the condom on impulse, wanting a memento, and she wasn't sure if he found her charmingly funny or entirely too bold. For the first time in her life she didn't know where she stood with a man, and it was driving her insane.

After a split second, he said, "I'll get the door. You get the condom."

Fortunately neither endeavor took long. When they met back in the center of the room Hunter removed her dress and tossed it aside. "This time—" with a firm hand he gently pushed her down to the plush carpet and a thrill rushed through her "—I'm in charge." He kept pressing until she was lying back, and then he slipped off her thong.

Throat tight, body aching for him, she watched Hunter take off his tux, starting with the coat, bow tie, and then his shirt. The sight of the finely honed torso—the one he'd placed between her and her dad after her father's insult—left her dying to take control. The acute need to worship lean muscle, warm skin and the hard, protective planes of his chest was strong. But when he shed his pants, was naked, his erection visible in all its glory, her heart pumped so hard she feared it would break free from her chest and flop to the floor.

Maybe it was a good thing he was taking the lead.

He knelt and lifted her leg, kissing her ankle. He nipped his way higher, scraping his teeth across her skin, palms soothing the fire his mouth left behind. When he reached her inner thigh, with a quick dart of his tongue he licked the nub between her legs, and a sensual jolt shocked every cell.

Before she could catch her breath he moved his attention to the other leg, giving it equal time. As his teeth nipped up her second thigh she closed her eyes, body humming, nerves straining, and arched to meet him. His lips landed on her center again and lingered, sending hot pleasure rushing through her. She gripped the thick carpet, a moan escaping her lips and sweat dotting her temples.

Time hovered, her mind expanding even as her muscles contracted, focusing on the point where Hunter's lips, teeth and tongue brought her to an ecstasy that washed everything away. There was no yesterday to regret. No tomorrow to worry about. Only the beautiful way Hunter made her feel.

Mouth between her legs, he worked his sensual magic, pushing her closer to the brink, so close to climax her whole body tensed.

He drew back and, crushed, she let out a cry. *"Wait."*

"You'll have to," he said, and calmly rolled on the condom. And then, eyes on hers, he shifted up her body. Instinctively she welcomed him. He arched between her thighs, going deep. Relief shuddered through her and she shifted to absorb more of him, meeting him thrust for thrust. There was no doubt. No uncertainty or distrust. Just a desire strong enough, sure enough, to push aside all the worries.

Heart pumping in her chest, hair damp at her neck, she closed her eyes as their hips strained against each other, her release just moments away.

This time when he pulled out her eyes flew open and Carly clutched his shoulders, speechless as he began to kiss his way down her neck to her collarbone. She found her voice, frustrated and flabbergasted. "What are you do—?"

His mouth landed on a nipple, eliciting a sharp hiss, cutting off her words. He nipped and kissed, as if relishing her flavor, and the sounds of her soft cries filled the room. Gradually she grew louder, spurring him on as his lips traced a path down her abdomen. He licked the tiny dip at her navel, drawing out a groan from Carly before he continued down. When his lips landed back on the sensitive center between her legs she called out his name. He lingered, apparently taking delight in pushing her higher, until she was close again, so close to completion she almost felt it.

Once more, before she could peak, he swooped up her body and drove deep between her legs. Arching his hips, he took all he could, and this time her body's response bordered on frantic. She let out a sob, the pleasure and need so great she dug her nails into his back, her legs aiding his thrusts as their hips bucked in unison. Tears of frustration burned her lids. The intensity of his gaze and the dark, determined look on his face shoved her closer to the edge. She began to whimper. And his movements, though controlled, grew carnal. Rough. Primal.

Mind spinning, muscles straining, she marveled at his strength. At the hard body that pushed her to the brink, exposing her even as he held her close. The hips that drove her closer to a dangerous ledge, his arms providing security.

Laying her open even as he protected.

Until she burst through the barrier, crying out from the force of her orgasm. And clung to Hunter as he joined her, the quake shaking her body with a ferocity that rocked the very foundation of her world.

"Looks like that cloud is bringing rain," Abby said.

From the lounge chair beside her, Carly shaded her eyes from the glare. "I think we'll be fine," she said, staring at the single gray ball of fluff blotting the horizon.

The noontime sun sparkled in the brilliant blue Miami sky—clear except for the single offending cloud—and the lingering cold weather added a slight nip to the breeze. The utilitarian concrete rooftop of Carly's apartment building was strictly for maintenance access. It wasn't as nice as her multimillion-dollar childhood home overlooking the Atlantic. But Carly had added a few potted ferns, along with some used patio furniture, and with the city sprawled out in front

she considered it heaven. After about a week of wondering
where she stood with Hunter Philips, right now she needed
the tranquil haven.

"Pete Booker asked me to spend the weekend with him,"
Abby said.

Carly sent her a pleased grin. "And you said he wouldn't
ask you out after the last date."

"Yeah, well..." Abby picked at her black leggings and
smoothed her hand down the dark top with sleeves that flared
at the wrists. "There's always a chance he'll change his mind."

Carly studied her friend, her tone soft. "Not every relationship ends in catastrophe, Abby."

"All mine have." She twisted to face Carly, her black hair
in pigtails. "And unless you're holding out on me," she shot
her a meaningful look, "so have yours." Carly resisted the
urge to wince at the truth, and Abby went on. "Speaking of
questionable relationships—have you heard from Hunter?"

Carly's heart took a tumble. "Not since my dad's party."

"You'd think by now he'd, like...you know...actually ask
you out on a date."

Carly slunk down in her chair and pulled her sun visor
lower, shading her eyes. Too bad she couldn't block her con-
cerns as easily.

Confused, emotionally and physically exhausted from the
evening, the moment she and Hunter had rejoined the party
Carly had left. And she'd spent the last seven days wondering what Hunter would have done if she hadn't begged him
to make love to her. No longer sidetracked by his disturbingly delicious presence, it was impossible not to scold herself for continuing to pursue a man who didn't trust her.
Wasn't it enough to beat her head against the stubborn attitude of her father?

Must she continue to seek approval from those who
doubted her the most?

After deliberating for hours, she'd decided it was time to cut her losses. Apparently self-control was impossible when it came to Hunter. She had no choice but to face him on the third show, but she could stay far, far away from him until then.

As plans went, it was all she had.

"And speaking of catastrophes," Abby said in a grim tone, as if she'd read her mind, "you put a lot of effort into getting approval to write a piece on Hunter Philips. Now that our boss has finally said yes what are you going to tell her?"

Carly stared at her friend, and tension flooded her faster than she could reason away her fears. The look on Abby's face reflected all the dark predictions she'd made from the beginning. For the first time Carly feared her friend wasn't so much a pessimist as a realist.

And then Hunter's voice came from behind. "Hello, Carly."

Carly's heart plunged to her stomach, and Abby shot from her chair, mumbling excuses about rain, getting wet, catching pneumonia, dying and burning in hell as she made a beeline for the exit. Gathering her courage, Carly twisted in her seat to watch Hunter approach, clad in a sleek leather jacket, pants and a dress shirt. He looked fresh and rested, but she hadn't slept well for a week, reliving every moment with Hunter in her father's house.

He sank into the lounge chair vacated by Abby. "Nice view," he said, nodding at the city.

She doubted he was here to take in the sights. "How did you find me?"

"I saw your car in the garage and asked your neighbor where you were."

They stared at each other, and silence fell. After her tumultuous family reunion, not to mention their sizzling interlude in the study, she was unable to play games or pretend to be polite—her nerves were too raw for her usual charm.

She needed peace—which meant she needed him to leave. "What do you want, Hunter?" she said bluntly.

His voice was low, sincere. His blue eyes warmer than normal, their usual frost…gone. "I have to attend a conference in Las Vegas this weekend." His gaze was steady. "I'd like you to come with me."

Stunned, Carly bit her lower lip, struggling to adjust to the development. A weekend together didn't exactly jive with her goal of avoiding the man. Unfortunately she loved how he made her feel, and it went well beyond what he did to her in bed—not that they'd technically made it to a bedroom yet. A part of her was tempted to risk a bigger piece of her heart just to spend more time with him. Another part was scared as hell.

She really should refuse.

Heart thumping with the force of a thousand bass drums, she tried to play it cool and keep it light. She hiked a teasing brow. "It won't make me go easy on you on the show."

"I'm not afraid," he said, his faint smile utterly seductive.

Her resolve slipped a bit. "I'm still going to challenge you to pull The Ditchinator."

"I can handle it."

Her heart thudded, and her attempt at keeping it light died. "My boss has accepted my request to do a story on you." If that didn't get him to bolt, nothing would. And, though his body didn't move, his whole demeanor tensed as her words hung in the air.

"And if I refuse?" he said.

"It doesn't matter. We've slept together. I can't write it now."

He cocked his head. "Have you told your boss?"

Ah, yes. There *was* that little hiccup to contend with. Carly briefly closed her eyes as panic threatened to overtake her, but she fought it back. After months of chasing Sue about potential story ideas, and having spent a considerable amount of time pointing out the advantages of a story on Hunter—including his current popularity with the local press—now she had to figure out a way to tell her boss no. Short of claiming the public's interest had waned, or sharing that she'd slept with the man, she was out of ideas. The first was an obvious lie. The second could get her fired. Again.

Swallowing past the boulder in her throat, she met his gaze. "I'll tell her soon."

She just had to figure out how. Sleeping with him hadn't been the smart thing to do. But the enigmatic Hunter Philips had captured her attention where every other man had barely registered a "huh." And now he was here offering her a whole weekend with him.

A gift that could eventually bite her in the backside.

Delay tactics were in order. "What kind of conference?" she said.

"The largest hacker convention in the US. Hackers, security experts, even law enforcement attend to keep up with the latest tricks. I've gone to Defcon every year since I was a teen."

"Did your dad take you?"

Hunter let out a laugh. Stunned, Carly watched amusement roll off the man. "No, my dad's not into technology—though he *is* retired FBI," he said. "His dad was a Fed too."

The news explained a lot. "It's in your blood?"

"Absolutely. But not in the same way. Dad is old school, and doesn't like reliance on computers, so we've had a few heated debates in our time," he said dryly, giving the impression he was understating the truth. And she knew a lot about heated family debates. "But…" His expression grew thoughtful as he looked out over the city. "Even when we disagreed about everything else," he said, and then turned to face her, "the law and justice were two subjects where we always saw eye to eye."

She tipped her head. "Fidelity. Bravery. Integrity…" she mused softly. Would that *her* family mantra was so noble. "You grew up living the FBI motto."

A dark look flitted across his face, and he shifted his gaze away. "Not exactly."

Surprised, Carly crossed her arms. "You mean you *haven't* always lived the life of a justice-seeking action hero?" Silence followed, and her teasing statement grew awkward as his expression remained serious, his eyes studying the skyline. Curiosity now at full throttle, Carly said, "Do tell."

Hunter didn't move, as if weighing his options, and it was a full minute before he finally spoke. "Booker and I grew up together," he said. "Being an eccentric genius works as an adult, but back then he was the target of every clique in school."

Given what she knew of Pete Booker, the news wasn't a surprise. She lifted her brows, waiting for him to go on. Instead she had to prompt him. "And…?"

"And until we became friends I never lifted a finger to stop them," he said bluntly, finally meeting her gaze, his eyes heavy with regret. "Our sophomore year, the wrestling team tossed him in a Dumpster while I stood by and did nothing." He let out a soft, self-derisive scoff. "That's just one of several instances Booker has never mentioned, though I'm sure he remembers." Hunter gazed out over the skyline, as if the memories were too distasteful to contemplate. "I know I do…"

Carly stared at his profile, remembering the teen years she'd spent clashing with her father. "Adolescents do stupid things," she said. "How did you two wind up friends?"

"When we were assigned a joint project in high school we discovered a mutual interest in computers. Booker invited me along to the Defcon conference with him and his dad." He smiled. "And I learned that, along with his bizarre and occasionally wicked sense of humor, he's a really good guy."

"I bet that changed things at school," she said softly.

He shot her a look with the remnants of a lethal intensity that had no doubt kept others in line. "After that I never stood by and did nothing again," he said. "No matter who was the target."

Carly's heart melted. Hunter was the most honorable man she'd ever met. With Carly he had put up the good fight, and probably still would. But when it came to push or shove the good guy inside of him always won out. Deep down, where it really counted, he *did* embody the FBI motto.

What would it be like to have a man like that in her life?

She blinked back the rushing rise of emotion, the last of her resolve slipping away. "So…" she said. "When do we leave for Vegas?"

Hunter's expression eased as he reached out and traced a line along her arm. The touch was simple. Warm. And clear in its intent. "Tomorrow night," he said, and he lifted his slate-blue gaze back to hers, sending a thrill skittering up her spine.

She wondered what the noise was, until she realized it was herself trying to breathe.

The light in his eyes made them breathtakingly beautiful as he said, "Right after I spend the day teaching you how to handle my gun."

CHAPTER NINE

JIM'S INDOOR FIRING RANGE was busy, but the shots fired by the patron in the adjacent booth were muted by the thick concrete walls and Hunter's headset. Fortunately the heavy earphones they were wearing had a built-in microphone system that allowed him to hear Carly's voice, including her sarcasm, albeit with a tinny sound.

"Is this how you dazzle the women you date?" she said.

His lips twitched as he reloaded the gun. "I wouldn't think you'd be so easily impressed."

"It's hard not to be. You handle that weapon like it's an extension of yourself." She nodded in the direction of the distant bullseye where Hunter's shots had been recorded electronically. "You hit dead center every time. I'm feeling inadequate already."

"You have other areas of expertise," he said, amused when she rolled her eyes.

Like holding a new firearm for the first time, it felt odd having her here—not necessarily wrong, just…different. And most likely that feeling would return when they boarded the plane for Las Vegas tonight. He'd never taken a woman to Defcon before—his days there were strictly his own. Mandy had wanted to come along once, but he'd talked her out of it, convinced she would have been bored. But this time he'd

hated the idea of a weekend without seeing Carly. A disturbing trend it was best not to think too much about.

Concentrating on his current agenda was a better course
of action.

Hunter attempted a serious tone as, with his nine-milli-
meter Glock 17 in hand, he stepped behind her. Both of them
were facing the bullseye. "The safety is on, but remember
to always treat a gun as if it's loaded and the safety is off."
Mindful of her inexperience, he shifted closer, until he could
feel the heat from her skin. Serious became harder to maintain. "Now, square your hips and shoulders with the target."
He placed one hand on her hip, ignoring the delicious curve,
and checked her alignment as he passed her the weapon.

Arms extended, she gripped the gun as he'd instructed
earlier, and targeted the bullseye at the far end of the room.
Her hip shifted beneath his hand, and her voice was almost...
distracted. "Are you intentionally trying to mess me up?"

Biting back a smile, he said, "You're drifting down." He
reached around her to lift her wrists—a pseudo-embrace
from behind.

"Not. Helping."

"Just ignore me," he said, amused even as he tried to
apply the advice to himself. Arms extended alongside hers,
he leaned in to help her aim, his mouth at the level of her temple. The scent of citrus and the feel of her skin set his heart
thumping dangerously. "Look down the barrel and square
the sights with the target."

"I'm trying," she muttered. "And you'd think I'd get a few
lessons *before* I learned to deal with distractions."

His lips quirked. "You're a quick study. I'm sure you'll
have no problem. Now," he said, forcing the serious tone back
to his voice. He lightly gripped her elbows. "Brace for the
kickback. When you're ready, release the safety, check your
alignment again, and slowly pull the trigger."

She did as told, and the gun fired with a loud bang. Carly didn't squeal, jump, or even flinch at the discharge. Instead she fired off two more shots in quick succession. When the echoing sound and the smell of gunpowder cleared, Carly finally spoke.

"Wow," she said with an awed tone. "The kickback is a shocker."

Maintaining her position, she turned her head to look at him curiously. Her lips close to his were heating his blood.

"Does the surprise ever go away?" she said.

"You get used to it," he said, doubting the same was true of touching Carly. He dropped his hands to her waist and shifted, his length now molded to hers from hip to thigh. Desire shot like bottle rockets, as forceful as any kickback from a gun. All parts of him tense and ready for action, he had to force his mind to focus. "You did a nice job."

"Purely a credit to your detailed instructions." She faced the bullseye. "You must spend a lot of time here."

"Every Friday morning before work."

After a pause, arms extended, gun aimed at the target, Carly fired off several mores shots before she turned her head again. Her bold gaze was mere inches from Hunter's. "You never did tell me why you still come."

He searched for an appropriate reply. In the end, a version of the truth seemed best. "I guess a part of me still misses my old job," he said, the understatement sitting uneasily in his gut.

After slipping the safety on the now empty Glock, Carly lowered her arms, twisting her shoulders to face him. "So why did you go into private business?"

The old resentment surged, and he stepped to the side and took his gun from her, careful to keep his tone even. "It was time to move on."

"It's a far cry from catching criminals."

"It's a living."

"So is writing columns about art gallery openings, night-clubs…" her lips quirked "…and trendy apps." A brief moment of amusement passed between them.

"Not your favorite kinds of assignments?" he said, holding her gaze.

"No." Her grin grew wistful. "I'm a nosy reporter that prefers people to facts."

"Who also has a tendency to get herself into trouble," he said dryly.

"I think that's why you've been following me around," she said. "I've decided I'm an outlet for your overdeveloped need to safeguard others. A need that hasn't been met since you left the FBI."

"That isn't the reason I joined the force."

Her eyes grew serious. "So what *did* you get out of it?"

He studied her for a moment, weighing his response carefully. But ultimately the unvarnished truth came out with more heat than he'd intended. "I got to catch the criminal bastards."

Either his tone or the words—or perhaps both—brought a smile of comprehension to Carly's lips. "You liked to out-maneuver them." Her grin grew bigger. "You liked the excitement of the chase."

The dull ache was back, and he clutched the handle of the Glock tight as she went on.

"Why don't you go back?" Her words were spoken innocently, as if it was that simple.

But innocence hadn't helped him much.

Gut churning, Hunter turned to the tables lining the wall, opening a gun case. There was a time when he'd been confident it would. When Truth, Honor and Justice—and all the other noble qualities he'd been raised to believe in—had meant something.

"That isn't my job anymore." He jettisoned the empty clip from the Glock, his back to Carly. "I have a business to run. Responsibilities. Commitments. And Booker hates the business end of things." Hunter reached for another magazine to load. "We should get on with the lesson."

He could sense her eyes on his back as she said, "You haven't told him how you feel?"

His jaw tensed, and he stared down at the second clip clutched tightly in his hand, struggling against the emotion that had been eating at him for months.

Instead, he said, "I owe him."

Her tone was skeptical. "Because of something that happened back when you were a kid?"

"No," he said firmly. "It's more than that." Because the friend who'd proved himself through thick and the worst of the thin deserved better. With a hard shove of his palm, he popped the clip into the Glock, loading the gun for another round. "When I told Booker I was leaving to start my own business I asked him if he wanted to quit his consulting work for the FBI and join me. He didn't hesitate."

"I'm sure he left because he wanted to."

"You're right. He isn't a martyr." Checking the safety, he set the gun on the table and turned to stare at her. "But he *is* a loyal friend who deserves better than getting dumped with an aspect of the job that he has no interest in."

"How do you know he's not interested?" she said.

"You've met him," he pointed out. "He isn't what you'd call a people person."

"Hiding behind his computer doesn't necessarily mean he doesn't want to branch out. Maybe he just needs a little encouragement. And if his interaction with Abby is anything to go by," she said, a wry grin forming, "he might not need much encouragement at all."

Unconvinced, he didn't respond, hoping if he said nothing they'd move on to the task at hand.

Instead, she said, "Look, Hunter. I know how loyal you are to Pete. And I know you feel some sort of obligation. But you need to be honest with him. You can't let a ridiculous sense of duty rule the rest of your life." She lowered her voice, but not its intensity. "Are you happy?"

He swore under his breath and turned to stare at Carly's electronic score. As was fitting for a first attempt, her aim was way off. In her assessment of him, unfortunately, she was unerringly accurate. "No," he said, blowing out a breath. "I'm not happy. I'm bored."

He'd never admitted to the feeling out loud—though he'd thought it, *felt* it acutely, every day.

"Talk to him," she said. "Tell him how you feel. Work something out. Establish a new set of rules for your band-of-brothers, bro-code mentality." She laid a hand on his arm. "A real friend will be able to handle the truth."

Torn, he nodded down at the gun on the table and lifted a brow. "Do you want to shoot another clip or not?"

She paused, pursing her lips and studying him for a moment. "Are you going to distract me again?"

His grin returned. "I'll do my best."

She smiled back. "Then count me in."

"In retrospect, the *Star Trek* convention tickets I sent you as a bribe weren't so wrong," Carly said with a teasing smile.

"This is where sci-fi meets reality." Hunter gazed around the crowded Las Vegas convention hall at the attendees of the Defcon conference—the annual pilgrimage destination for hackers. At a table in front of them participants with laptops were competing to see who could hack into the most servers in under an hour. So far Booker was in the lead, Abby cheering him on from behind.

Hunter nodded his head in the direction of his friend. "I never did tell you that Booker enjoyed the *Star Trek* convention in my place."

Carly shifted closer to Hunter's side, setting his body humming. "Which reminds me of something I wanted to discuss with you," she said. Her citrusy scent enveloped him, bringing back sensual memories of the past two days, and he hoped she was thinking what he was thinking. Carly said, "Have you talked to him yet?"

He sighed. Apparently her mind wasn't in sync with his. "I don't want to talk to my partner. He isn't nearly as pretty as you."

She narrowed her eyes in amused suspicion. "You're using delaying tactics."

"No." A grin hijacked his mouth, and he leaned closer. "I'm enjoying my weekend."

Which was true. He hadn't enjoyed himself this much since... He paused, trying to remember. Intellectually it should have been when he was with Mandy. But he was quite sure that he had never felt as alive in Mandy's presence as he did in Carly's. It wasn't just her smart, sassy ways, or that the sex was better—though that was a definite plus. Carly made the funny funnier and the interesting more interesting.

He would certainly never look at *Hamlet* the same way again.

"And, by the way, the next time you plan on sending a gift as a bribe," he went on, "I do have a list of preferences." He had several—and all of them involved a beautiful woman who had taken his life by storm. The timbre of his voice gave away the under-the-sheets direction of his thoughts. "Do you want me to share my favorites with you?"

Carly's quasi-serious expression melted into a welcoming one, and Hunter's body registered its approval. He loved her infectious enthusiasm. He loved how she'd embraced the playful side of the conference, cheering on the participants that succeeded at the annual "Spot the Fed" game.

As a teen, for him the conference had been about fun. As an FBI agent and then a security specialist Hunter had focused entirely on the business aspect. But Carly had convinced him to enter the "Crack the Code" competition. She'd even lured him away from a lecture for a lunchtime rendezvous in their room yesterday. And he hadn't been getting much sleep at night, either…

"You have a list of gifts that won't get sent back to me?" she said as she stepped closer, and he wondered if she could hear his heart thumping appreciatively in response. "This I'd like to hear," she went on. "Because I still have that secret decoder ring you returned."

"You kept it?"

"As a memento of our first show."

"I hope you still have the dress," he said in a low voice.

"I do," she said with a seductive smile. "And I brought it with me."

"Good. I can finally live out my fantasy of making love to you with it on."

"I don't think it will fit you," she said silkily.

Hunter laughed, and then leaned in to whisper in her ear, savoring her scent. "I'd give it a whirl in private, if that's what you wanted."

"Oh…" She pulled back until they were face to face, and her gaze turned decidedly warmer. "I definitely want."

The look seared him, frying the very marrow of his bones. But the heat in her eyes suggested her statement wasn't just about the dress, or even the ridiculous notion of him putting it on. It was almost as if she hoped for more, and it was shocking to realize they might have moved beyond desire and into something else.

It was easy to get lost in the sensual web she wove so

easily, because his body had begun to insist it was time for another noontime rendezvous. But still… "Do you want to know what I really want?" he said.

"Yeah." She lifted her chin, as if ready for anything—and she always was. "I do."

For a heart-pounding moment he tried to figure out the truth. What did he want? When the answer wouldn't come, he dropped his gaze to her legs, plenty exposed in the shorts she was wearing. "I want to know if they make shorts any shorter than that."

"Of course," she said breezily. "They're called bathing suits. But I don't think I'll be allowed in the convention hall wearing one."

"I don't think anyone would complain."

She looked at the crowd that consisted of people of all ages. Most were excited to meet like-minded people, engaged in conversations she probably couldn't understand. "I don't think anyone would *notice*."

His smile grew bigger. "Except me."

She smoothed a hand over his button-down shirt with a light in her eyes and the sassy self-assurance that set his soul on fire. "Your focus is one of the things I like about you."

Hunter gazed down at Carly, and beyond the intense desire that was growing by the second there was a sense of rightness, a light of possibility, that refused to go away. The feeling had been coming with greater regularity, and while he didn't necessarily trust it, the wholehearted, unwavering resistance that used to accompany the emotion was growing less acute. In truth…it was beginning to fade quite a bit.

Which in and of itself should have been concerning.

But right now he was simply going to enjoy himself. "And the other things you like about me?"

"I'm rather fond of your gun." Her grin grew bigger. "Your ability to remain cool under pressure. And I like how you wear that white hat." She glanced up at his hatless head and then returned his gaze. The teasing light in her eyes faded a trace as she grew more serious and dropped her hand from his chest. "Why haven't you talked to Pete yet?"

Hunter stifled a groan and turned to face the competitors at the table that included his partner, the guilt weighing him down. It would have been easier to ask for more time to pursue other interests—to break free of the stifling responsibility of keeping the business going—if it didn't feel like such a noose around his neck. But right now his life felt, if not perfect, as close to happy as he could remember. And he didn't want to ruin it with thoughts of his lingering dissatisfaction at work.

Hunter put an arm around Carly's waist and pulled her closer to him. "I'll discuss it with him when the time is right." His hand drifted lower, as if to hold her hip, but he kept right on going until his palm cupped the outside of her upper thigh. The feel of silky skin brought the desire back tenfold, not to mention some outstanding memories. "Currently I have other things on my mind. Like yesterday afternoon..." His thumb smoothed across her thigh, slipping under her shorts and tracing the edge of her panties at her hip. The crowd around them blocked most everyone's view of his hand.

Though she parted her lips, as if to catch her breath, her lids narrowed just enough to let him know she was trying to continue her discussion. The flush on her cheeks gave her difficulty in focusing away.

"I *could* go discuss business with my partner." He leaned in and spoke at her ear, pushing aside his frustration with the topic in favor of overwhelming desire. "Or we could go back to the hotel room and start working our way down my list..."

When she didn't move or speak, he straightened a touch to look down at her face, and the look of pure need in her eyes was his undoing. His fingers discreetly stroked her thigh, and the energy flowing between them could have lit the LED light display that covered the massive expanse of ceiling.

"Still susceptible to a pretty face, I see," a man said from behind.

The familiar voice from his FBI days plunged Hunter's heart headlong into blackness, snuffing out the light in his good mood, and his fingers gripped Carly's hip. In a blinding flash intense resentment flared. The sharp taste of bitterness. The bite of betrayal filling his heart.

Carly's wide-eyed look helped him regain his composure. Through sheer force of will Hunter transferred the pressure in his grasp on Carly's hip to the muscles in his jaw.

"Hello, Terry," Hunter said as he turned to face his old colleague.

Stunned, Carly took in the cold look that frosted Hunter's eyes—worse than any she'd seen to date—and a chill crept up her spine at the dark emotion exuding from his every cell. He dropped his hand from her hip and she instantly missed the heat.

Since they'd been in Las Vegas he'd been relaxed. Not coiled, tense, ready for trouble at a moment's notice. But now the reserve was back, and it was shocking how fast the old wall could so thoroughly, and so quickly, be thrown back up. She sensed the tension, the seething energy around the two men.

The redhead's buzz cut barely concealed his scalp, but it was the gleam of smug satisfaction in his eyes as he looked at Hunter that left her wary. Despite the chatter in the convention hall, the ominous silence between the two threatened to engulf them—until the newcomer decided to put an end to it.

The freckle-faced gentleman stuck out a hand at Carly. "Terry Smith," he said.

She mumbled her name and returned the shake out of courtesy, dropping his hand as soon as polite.

"Old FBI buddy of Hunter's, from his days with the Cyber Division," the man finished, though Carly doubted the word "buddy" was an accurate description. "Do you hack, or are you into security?"

"Neither," she said. "I'm a journalist."

The slight widening of Terry Smith's eyes registered just how much of a shock her profession was to him, vaulting her reporter's curiosity to lunar levels. But as he slid a sideways glance at Hunter, Terry's smirk grew bigger. Carly's heart flinched in preparation for what she sensed was about to become a worse situation.

"What is with your fascination for members of the press?" Terry's gaze touched back on Carly's. "Though who can blame you? She's hot too…"

Carly's heart tripped and fell, landing painfully on his use of the word "too." Hunter's face went glacier, rivaling the polar icecaps for frigid first place, and the menacing look that crossed his face robbed her of the ability to function. Hunter took a half-step forward and Terry's eyes briefly flickered with alarm. But whatever Hunter had intended was stopped by the sudden appearance of Pete at his side. His friend placed a restraining hand on his shoulder.

More mocking than holding real humor, Pete's boyish grin was aimed at Terry. "How ya handling that alcoholic habit of yours, Terry?"

The agent's face registered relief before he narrowed his eyes suspiciously at Pete. "Funny how it works every year at Defcon. My hotel room gets charged with another guest's consumption of alcohol." He paused and crossed his arms, the generic dark suit pulling tight across his narrow shoulders, his words thick with meaning. "Almost as if someone hacks the hotel computer and sends the bar bill from their room to mine."

Hunter's clenched jaw loosened a fraction, as if he was amused by the indirect accusation. "There are a lot of hackers at this conference with nothing better to do than stir up trouble."

Pete tipped his head in false sympathy. "Yeah, and you Fed boys will always be a target."

"It's a big bill too," Terry said, clearly finding little humor in the prank. "Hundreds of dollars."

"Pretty prohibitive with your salary," Hunter said.

"I guess whoever it is must be throwing a party," Pete added.

"Probably all in your honor," Hunter said. The FBI agent's lips tightened, and his grim look only got worse when Hunter went on, "Rumor has it every year the bill gets paid anonymously."

"Yeah," Terry said softly, his eyes glittering with accusation. "It doesn't undo the illegal act, though." He shifted his gaze between Hunter and Pete, as if looking for clues to the crime in their faces and trying to determine which one was doing the hacking and which one was paying the bill. "And if I ever catch the person doing it," Terry said, "I'm bringing him down."

"Lighten up, Terry," Pete said with a laugh and a playful slap of the agent's shoulder. "It's probably a couple of kids having fun at your expense." Pete's smile developed an edge. "Of course, with your poor skills, whoever it is should consider themselves safe from detection."

The insult hung in the air, and none of the three men made a move, as if each was waiting to see what his adversary would do next.

"A few of us are meeting up at the bar tonight." Terry's gaze swept back to Carly. "If any of you guys want to catch

up, reminisce about old times…" his grin was positively de-
risive "…stop by." And, with that, he headed into the crowd.

Carly's mind twirled in the aftermath. It was too much
information to be processed quickly, and as she watched the
FBI agent walk away a million questions swirled in her head.
Her curiosity was so sharp she couldn't decide where to start.
With the reporter comment? With the history of the animos-
ity between the three men? Or perhaps with who was hacking the hotel computer and stiffing Terry with the bar bill?

But when she turned to speak with Hunter…he was gone.

Hunter sat on a chair in the corner of his hotel room, thick
curtains blocking all but a thin swath of the dying embers
of the setting sun. After his aimless wander along the noisy
chaos of the well-lit Vegas strip the dim light and silence of
the hotel room was a relief. Out on the sidewalk he'd passed
three Elvis impersonators, four superheroes, and a gold-
painted human statue of Midas. Carly would have loved every
one of them. He shouldn't have left her so abruptly, but he'd
needed time to regain control of his anger.

Nursing the same bourbon he'd poured when he'd returned
to the room an hour ago, Hunter stared across the posh pent-
house suite. In his days as an FBI agent, a government em-
ployee on a limited budget, he'd been assigned one of the
cheapest rooms on the bottom floor. Now he could afford the
best of the best at the top. A massive room, lavish with plush
furniture, thick carpeting, and a well-stocked bar that deserved someone who drank more than him. Since his drinking binge following Mandy's defection his taste for alcohol
had waned.

Running into Terry had triggered an avalanche of troubled
emotions Hunter had battled for eight years. At one time the
salary slur he'd tossed at Terry would have left Hunter satisfied, knowing that he could buy and sell the man's life ten

times over and never pull a financial muscle. But in reality it was an empty win. Hunter hadn't minded the cheap rooms, the basic government-issue cars, or the limiting lifestyle of a G-man on a G-man's salary. The work, the satisfaction of his job had supplied him with all that he'd needed: a sense of purpose. A calling he believed in. And—the real chocolate frosting on the plain vanilla cake—the thrill of outwitting the crooks and beating them at their own game.

Until his integrity had been called into question.

The acrid memories of those dark days burned—the shame, frustration and humiliation of going to work while the agency's Office of Professional Responsibility had scrutinized his life. Being investigated like the criminals he'd been tracking for two years.

He clutched the cold tumbler in his hand, bitterness twining around his every cell, tightening its grip. Choking him. And twisting the knife still buried in his back.

A rustling came from the hall and Hunter tensed, not yet fit for human interaction. But the sound of a card swiping the outer lock was followed by the door opening, and a soft click as it closed.

Carly.

CHAPTER TEN

RELIEVED she'd finally found him, Carly paused, caught between her incessant need to know what had just transpired between Hunter and his old colleague and her intense longing to ease the expression on his face. She'd seen the Hope Diamond once, and his eyes resembled it now. Blue. Hard. Frozen. Though hope was hardly an apt description. There was such an underlying sense of…emptiness about him.

After the last few days with Hunter it was hard to adjust back to the elusiveness he'd exuded in the beginning. But the wall had returned, taller and stronger than ever, and his expression was sealed off—tighter than any super computer responsible for national secrets.

"After you left the convention hall," she said from across the room, "I came back here looking for you."

"I went for a walk."

She paused, refusing to be deterred by his less than approachable tone. "Agent Terry Smith is an ass."

"Yes, he is." He didn't even look at her when he went on. "He always has been."

"You two never got along?"

There was a pause before he spoke. "He considered me a rival at work."

Her eyes dropped to the glass in his hand, as she decided

how to proceed. "Is that bourbon you're drinking going on your hotel bill…or obnoxious Agent Smith's?"

The hardness in his expression lightened a touch, and the frosty look in his eyes thawed half a degree. "It's going on mine."

Encouraged, she crossed the last of the distance between them. "I figured as much," she said, tossing her purse on the bed as she passed by on her way to Hunter. "Pete's the one who's been hacking the hotel computer every year and switching the bar bills, isn't he? And you've been anonymously paying the tab." The scenario fit with everything she knew about the two. The eccentric mathematical genius and—ever the white-hat-sporting defender—his brilliant and fiercely loyal friend smoothing the way.

His brow crinkled in the faintest of amusement. "A little continued rivalry would be understandable, given our history. But hacking the hotel computer would be illegal," he said.

She came to a stop beside his chair, and something in the way he'd said the words, in his expression, made her question her assumption. "Are *you* the culprit?"

He finally looked up at her with a hint of a secretive smile on his face. "Why would I admit to a criminal act?"

Her heart untwisted and eased. She adored the look on his face and was relieved to see the barrier drop a fraction. But her curiosity climbed to heretofore unseen levels—and for her that was saying something.

"You're not going to tell me, are you?" she said.

"No," he said. "I'm not."

She fingered the strap of her dress, hesitating, but she had to ask. Although she suspected she knew the answer it was several seconds before she worked up the nerve. "Was your ex a reporter?"

Nothing changed in his demeanor, but his fingertips

blanched against his drink, as if crushing the glass. "Yes," he said. "She was."

The implications of the news were enormous. It explained a lot about his initial attitude toward her, and it opened up a slew of potential about what had happened between the couple. Was it more than just a girlfriend who had decided to move on? More than just a woman who'd changed her mind about a man she supposedly loved? Carly's thoughts spun with the possibilities.

She knew he wouldn't answer, but she tried anyway. "Were you ever going to tell me?"

The pause was lengthy. "Probably not."

His answer was more painful than she'd expected. "What happened?"

"It's not important," he said, his voice grim, and then he tossed back the last of his drink.

She blinked back the hurt and the growing sense of panic. Inviting her to the conference had seemed like a major step forward. Now she wasn't so sure. But there *had* to be hope, and the pain she sensed he'd buried for years currently outweighed her own. Her own need to heal his hurts, to tear down those barriers once and for all.

Exactly why she felt it so keenly wasn't a matter up for consideration. The last thing she wanted to do was examine just how much she needed to get back to the connection they'd shared the last few days. It had felt like a real relationship, not the over-him-in-forty-eight-hours kind. More like an intense, never-will-recover, want-to-be-with-him-forever kind.

The thought of this man walking away came perilously close to being frightening.

He carefully set his glass on a nearby table and looked up at her with an expression that squeezed her chest—utter bleakness, infused with a burning desire. A compelling combination that made his tone gruff. "Did you put that outfit on for me?"

Heart now rapping hard, she glanced down at the leopard print slip dress she'd worn the night of their first TV show. She'd put it on earlier, with the thought of teasing him into a better mood when she found him, but now it seemed inappropriate. And very, very wrong. The light in his eyes was encouraging, but the fatigue, the sense of emptiness he kept buried beneath it all, was unmistakable.

"Hunter," she said, looking down at him. "It's been a difficult day, and you're tired."

"I'm fine."

"Have you eaten?"

Eyes on hers, he clasped her wrist, his grip firm. "I'm not hungry."

Pulse pounding harder, her resolve melted a touch. "You need to rest. You need to eat—"

"No." Gaze intense, fingers around her wrist, he reached up and cupped her neck, bringing her head closer as he murmured roughly, "I need *you*."

Her heart went wild in her chest as his mouth claimed hers from below. His lips and tongue held a desperation that was about more than just sexual need. It was intense, yes. Hot too. But the demand in his mouth was like that of a drowning man who seemed intent on taking her down with him.

She loved the way he made her feel. Special. Worthy of a sacrifice. But right now it was as if he needed her as much as she needed him…

Okay, Carly. This is obviously more than just lust.

The disturbing thoughts, the fear of wanting too much, were shoved aside when his hands raked up her thighs and over her hips. The despair and dogged determination in his touch set her skin on fire until she was sure her mostly naked body beneath the fabric would scorch her dress from the inside out.

With his mouth on hers, his palms consuming her body, her own need grew urgent. She began to unbutton his shirt, fingers clumsy with emotion, embarrassed at just how much this meant to her. This wasn't about control or dominance. It was about surrender—not to each other, but yielding to the intense need they shared. She unfastened his bottom button and smoothed her hand across his chest, craving the feel of crisp hair, warm skin and hard muscle. Meeting his mouth, kiss for kiss, she tried to absorb every sensation. Afraid it would be over too soon.

Dying to draw out the moment of being so desperately needed by this man—as if he could never walk away—she pulled her head back and knelt beside him. Her fingers fumbled as she tried to unfasten his pants, and she let out a small, self-conscious laugh. "I hope I don't hurt you."

"I'm not afraid."

Carly's hands stilled as she stared up at him, her heart pumping in her chest. Because he scared the hell out of her. But the frank desire in his eyes gave her courage, so she pulled out his erection and lowered her mouth to take a taste. Hunter's low groan drove her on, and she loved the way his hand threaded through her hair, cupping her head. Not with a sense of power or control, but one of almost vulnerability. A moment where his wall was at its lowest point. No reserve. No guard. Just his need in her hands.

Her mouth and her touch grew bolder, more demanding. Her hands, lips and tongue smoothed their way along the soft skin covering the hard shaft. Satin covering steel. The protector, the coolly controlled man, poised and ready at a moment's notice.

The desperation in his tone was her undoing, his voice ragged. "Carly…"

Hearing his plea, she stood and reached for the hem of her dress.

"No," he said, his eyes burning into hers, his voice tight with desire. "Leave it on."

Slick with need, throbbing from the force of the desire coursing through her veins, she slid her thong down, kicked it aside and fetched a condom from her purse. Fear, hope, and a feeling that came too close to love twined tightly in her heart. She concentrated on Hunter's almost desperate grip on her thighs as she straddled his legs, sitting on his lap as she sheathed him in latex.

Pulse doing double time, her breathing too fast, she said, "You seemed more amused than affected the first time I wore this dress."

His words came out a throaty rumble. "I was affected." He bunched her dress to her hips and positioned her over him, leaving her holding her breath. "*Very* affected."

Helpless in his arms, she arched her back as he began to slide inside.

"God help me," he groaned, filling her inch by delicious inch as he went on. "I still am."

Try as he might, Hunter couldn't hold back the moan of pleasure as he entered Carly. Her body was more than ready. Beyond welcoming. Wrapping him in a warmth that was less about heat and more about alleviating the years of ache within. Overcome by the sensation, he paused for a moment. With him embedded deep inside her, she cupped his face for a kiss that was part healing balm, part all-consuming need, and a very big part an emotion he refused to name. She pulled her lips back a fraction, hands on his cheeks, her warm amber gaze locked with his, and he began to move.

Their hips rocked in unison, slow yet sure, as they sa-

vored every sensation. And Carly let out a sigh, her eyes
growing darker.

Somewhere along the way the teasing tones and the playful
challenge had been left far behind. All that remained was his
need to lose himself in Carly. The selfless way she matched
his rhythm, held his face and looked into his eyes, mended
the cracks he'd sworn were too massive to be repaired. The
doubts and misgivings he'd clung to in order to preserve his
sanity were slipping. His heart was now too large to be con-
tained in a cynical box. The woman was a seductive mix of
sassy strength and endearing vulnerability, but it was the
caring in her gaze that drew him in. Called him to wade further, venture deeper.

Death by drowning didn't seem a bad way to go, so long
as it was Carly he was submerged in.

Giving himself over to the sensation, he wrapped one arm
around her waist, the other hand low on her back, and closed
his eyes, burying his nose at her neck, immersing himself as
he succumbed to the spell she cast. Turning himself over to
the sensation, he basked in her citrus scent, her soft skin and
the emotion she shared so readily. So freely. And so honestly.

The unequivocal return of passion in her hips as they
met his urged him on. Every savoring thrust increased his
greed. Wanting to claim it all, to absorb the very essence of
this woman, he fisted his hands in her hair, raking his teeth
across the pulse pounding at her neck. His breath turned
ragged against her damp skin and she clung to him, each of
them lost in the other. Although he maintained the unhur-
ried pace, the slow, strong strokes of his shaft grew rough,
rugged. And needy.

Until Carly let out a soft cry.

The brutally frank need built higher. Both frightening in
its intensity and healing in its authenticity. Weakening him
and strengthening him at the same time. And as her cries of

surrender turned into a call of completion the start of her orgasm gave him a final push. He took the leap with her, following her off the cliff and plunging headlong toward the ocean.
And then the pleasure hit hard and closed over his head.

Well, it wasn't quite what she'd envisioned, but there was no
denying it now.

She was in love.

Carly's chest hitched on a painful breath as she lay next to
a sleeping Hunter, staring up at the ceiling of the hotel room.
For years she'd wondered how the emotion would feel—perhaps like double rainbows with pots of gold, or frolicking
unicorns, or any other number of mythical, magical things
she'd heard of through the years. It was supposed to leave
her believing she could leap tall buildings in a single bound,
not longing to hide out in a basement.

She'd expected to feel energized and ready to take on the
world, not left flattened in its wake.

Carly squeezed her eyes shut, blocking out the fear and
forcing her breaths to come at a more doable rate—one that
didn't make her feel quite so dizzy or panicky. She turned
her head to look at Hunter—which didn't help her light-
headed sense of anxiety either. The masculine edges of his
face looked relaxed in sleep, as did the sensual lips that had
minutes before consumed hers. This time had been different.
He had made love to her as if all the barriers were gone. As
if desperate to satisfy an emotional need via a physical one.

Or maybe that was her being naive again. Because sex
was just sex, and with Hunter it had always been good, so
what did it really mean?

Confused, she covered her eyes with her hand. Love hadn't
brought the kind of harmony and feel-good vibes she'd always
imagined. And how could she rely on a feeling of closeness

in bed to mean anything? Perhaps, for Hunter, it really was all about the physical?

But she couldn't get beyond the feeling that facing his old colleague had brought all the old memories to the surface. That he had turned to her in a moment of pain—trusting her to see him through, having faith in the two of them.

And maybe pots of gold and frolicking unicorns were real and waiting for her right outside the hotel room.

With a subdued sigh, her doubts and fears too loud to be silenced, she rolled out of bed and quietly changed into jeans and a T-shirt. She combed her hair, slipped out of the room, and wandered down the hallway and into an elevator, pushing the button for the ground floor. As she descended Carly stared at her reflection in the mirrored wall, looking for the radiant glow that women in love were supposed to emit.

But where was the inner peace? The empowering sense of resolve? Or, for God's sake, at least her usual confidence? According to the generally accepted unwritten rules of romance she was now supposed to be an *über*-strong, formidable woman, endowed with the heroic ability to overcome all manner of obstacles simply with the power of the love in her heart.

All she felt was an overwhelming sense that she was no closer to breaching Hunter's mighty defenses than she had been *before* she knew she'd taken the emotional fall—but now failing to lure him out of his shell wasn't just about his happiness, but hers too.

Because, with those cool blue eyes, there was no way of being certain about anything.

The elevator doors opened and Carly made her way into the lobby, coming to a stop beside the marble fountain in the center. Feeling lost, she scanned the elegant scene. And then she spied obnoxious agent Terry Smith at the lobby bar.

A wave of discomfort settled deep in her belly. No surprise

that he lacked the imagination to seek out one of the many Las Vegas establishments that offered more than canned elevator music, hardwood floors, and an elegance so subdued it bordered on bland, generic posh.

She chewed on her lip, staring at the agent. He might lack imagination, but one thing he *did* have was knowledge about Hunter's past. All those tidbits Hunter hadn't shared…like the fact his former girlfriend had been a reporter.

Her heart and her brain crashed into one another again, leaving her struggling to adjust.

That little nugget of news about his ex had been relentlessly chugging around in circles in Carly's mind since she'd first learned the truth. Was there a link between Hunter's break with his girlfriend and his reasons for quitting the FBI? So far she had considered the events to be unrelated, but now she had a strong suspicion they weren't. With his ex being a reporter, it made the incidents a whole lot more likely to be connected.

And why hadn't he trusted her enough to tell her?

The ache returned, leaving her feeling vulnerable, and suddenly her need to know overwhelmed everything. She didn't require the nitty-gritty details, she didn't want a blow-by-blow account—though she would have gladly accepted both from Hunter if he'd suddenly decided to quit hiding behind unbreachable emotional barricades. She just wanted the answer to one question: had Hunter's girlfriend been involved with the leak that had led to him leaving the FBI?

And the only way to find out was to ask. She stared at the redhead, his scalp gleaming beneath the buzz cut.

Don't do it, Carly. Don't do it.

But, damn it, Hunter's past was about more than just *his* life now. It was about hers too. Love might not endow her with superpowers, but it did provide one indisputable truth—he held her future happiness in his hands.

Fear gripped her, more powerful than ever before. Retreating to what she did the best—seeking out answers, nosing out the truth—was the only way she knew how to take back a little of the massive control that had just been handed to Hunter. He now held her heart on a platter.

With a renewed sense of determination, she headed in the direction of the agent.

As the hotel elevator descended, Hunter cursed himself for conking out so fast. The late nights had caught up with him, and while Carly had slept in to make up for lost sleep Hunter had been up early, attending lectures at the conference. Still, the lost shut-eye had been a small price to pay for making love to Carly. Tonight, even after they were done, he'd pulled her close, wanting to stay awake and enjoy the sensation that had permeated every muscle in his body, making them slack. Loose. Unrestricted by the tension that had kept him bound tight for so long he couldn't remember the last time he'd felt so relaxed. The deep feeling of contentment, of *rightness*, came from holding Carly close. From making love to the woman who had wormed her way under his skin in a way that he'd never thought possible.

With her quirky love for the bizarre, her sense of humor, and her sexy, spirited love of fun, Carly had charged into his life and powered his way into his heart in a matter of weeks. Despite all his efforts he'd fallen so fast he was still struggling from the force of the impact. Life without her in it had become unthinkable. And the way she'd made love to him tonight suggested she felt the same way.

So why had he woken up alone?

Eager to be near her again, even if it was to inhale the fresh scent of her skin, to feel the warmth of her body sleeping next to his, he'd left the room with one purpose in mind: to tell Carly how he felt. That the stark emptiness that had threatened to swallow him whole was now filled with the smell of citrus…and the smile of a woman that filled gaps in places he hadn't known there were holes.

When the elevator doors parted on the ground floor Hunter exited and headed into the lobby. Pleasure hit when he spied Carly leaning against the counter at the bar. But the sense of well-being crashed when he spied who sat opposite her…

Special Agent Terry Smith.

The sucker punch to the gut almost dropped him to his knees. The emotional hit was so hard it knocked the air from his chest.

Heart pumping painfully, Hunter stood, frozen, staring at the two of them as the familiar, nauseating swell of betrayal set fire to his previous lighthearted thoughts, incinerating them in an instant. There was only one thing the two of them had in common. Him. And Hunter was one hundred percent certain he was the topic of conversation.

Instantly several memories flashed through his mind: Carly using her blog to rake him over the coals—subsequently making him the current subject of interest for the Miami press. Carly winning her boss's approval to do an in-depth piece on Hunter. And Carly making love to him—the first two times leaving him wondering what she had to gain.

Until tonight, when it had felt so different, so raw, it had lulled him into a sexually induced state of lethargy. Yet when he'd woken…she was gone.

Now she was talking to his former colleague. A man who knew every sordid detail about Hunter being duped by another woman. The duplicity, the slur on his good name, and the humiliatingly degrading days of being the subject of an inquiry by the department he'd sworn to serve.

Why was she talking to the FBI agent?

Hunter couldn't see beyond the most obvious answer. His story.

His vision tunneled and the edges grew gray, enveloping him in a black cloak that cut off every thought outside of confronting Carly Wolfe.

"Here you are," Hunter said from behind her, his voice encrusted with frost.

If she'd been a cat, his tone would have shaved several lives from Carly. She turned, and the look on Hunter's face left her frigid, chilling her to the core. Her heart thumped hard, forcing the blood through her frozen veins at an astronomical rate.

Terry Smith responded before her mouth could locate her tongue. "Hunter, come join our party. And just to prove there are no hard feelings—" the agent's smile was empty "—I'll buy you a drink."

Hunter's gaze remained fixed on Carly. "I'm not interested."

Carly's heart pumped harder and the strained atmosphere grew taut, the air dense from the tension. Was the anger on his face directed at his old coworker...or her? She had the horrible sinking feeling she was the cause.

The agent's grin lacked humor. "After you've paid my mixed-up hotel bar bill all these years, I owe you several hundred rounds at least."

"You don't owe me a thing," Hunter said.

His emphatic words about the yearly prank again left Carly with the impression that Hunter had done the hacking and Pete had done the paying.

"Not even one bourbon for old times' sake?" Terry said.

"I didn't want to drink with you back then," Hunter said, his tone lethally even, "and I don't want to drink with you now."

The agent refused to shut up. "Come on, Hunter. All Carly's been doing is asking questions about you."

Hunter's face went dark, and Carly's heart sank like an anchor. She opened her mouth to refute Terry's exaggerated claim, but the agent went on.

"So it wasn't like I got to enjoy a nice chat with your girl-friend," he said, and the up-and-down perusal the man gave Carly came dangerously close to a leer.

Up until now he'd been almost pleasant, and certainly not inappropriate. Carly had the impression Terry's offensive look was more about making Hunter angry than anything else.

The agent's words as he went on confirmed her theory. "Tell me—is she worth it?" Terry said. "Maybe if I found the right angle she'd offer to sleep with *me* for a story too."

Before Carly could fully register the insult, Hunter's fist connected with the agent's chin with a loud snap. One moment Terry Smith was sitting on a barstool, and the next he was sprawled on the floor. The gasps from the guests were loud, and a waitress dropped her tray, shattering glasses on the hardwood floor. Silence followed. The whole room was shocked into momentary stillness.

The two bartenders rounded the bar and Hunter took a step back, hands raised in a non-threatening gesture. His gaze pivoted from Terry—still lying on the floor, rubbing his chin—back to Carly. "No need to remove me, gentle-men," Hunter said to the staff, his slate-blue gaze on hers, so empty the negative pressure threatened to suck the very life from Carly's soul. "I'm done here." And, with an air of finality, he swiveled on his heel, heading toward the lobby.

The murmurs of the guests at the bar returned as a bar-tender helped Terry to his feet. The agent was sullen as he angrily waved the help away. It took Carly all of eight seconds to recover fully from the incident before she took off across the lobby, chasing after Hunter's retreating form.

"What are you doing?" she said.

He didn't stop walking. "I'm leaving."

"Where are you going?"

He didn't slow his pace. "Home."

Her patience was rapidly growing slimmer. "What is your problem?"

"Apparently my ability to choose who I sleep with. Did you find out anything good?"

Frustrated, and more than a little annoyed, Carly struggled to keep up, her legs stretching to match the longer length of his. "I didn't get a chance to ask him much of anything. You barged in and dropped him with a lethal right hook before I got a chance."

"Sorry to ruin your interview."

Anger flared. "Damn it, Hunter," she said, grabbing his arm. But he was bigger and stronger and powered by a fury that was almost frightening. The momentum of his emotion and his strength carried them both forward as she clutched his arm and went on. "It wasn't an interview."

"Then why were you talking to him?"

She bit her lip, her steps still carried forward by her grip on his arm as he made his way to the elevator. Dismayed, she struggled for a way to explain.

Curiosity hadn't killed the cat, because death would have been too easy.

In the end, the truth was all she had. "I wanted to ask him a question."

He stopped to face her and shook off her arm, stepping closer. "What question?" His eyes were iced over, his face hard, and he looked so distant it was difficult to remember anything other than this coldly reserved Hunter.

"I wanted to know why you left the FBI," she said. He stared at her, as if sensing there was more. "And I wanted to know if your girlfriend had anything to do with it."

"You could have asked me."

"I *did* ask you, but you said it wasn't important."

"Sorry I wasn't cooperative enough for you. I didn't mean to ruin your plans. Or maybe this *was* your plan all along?"

Her patience lost so much weight it disappeared. "What the hell are you talking about?"

"Your plan to lull me into sleep with a good round of sex and then slip away to find Terry. Get the story you've wanted all along."

Carly was proud she didn't stomp her foot, and even more amazed she didn't slug him with her fist. But his jaw was so set, his expression so stony, she would have broken her hand while he would have hardly registered the tap to his face. Instead, hope died. Her heart burst. And her soul curled up in the corner and immediately began to lick its mortal wounds.

He'd made her feel worth protecting. But that was a reflection of him. That was who he was and what he did. It was no reflection of his belief in her. He'd faced down two supposed thugs because he would shield anyone who was threatened. He'd slugged a man because of a vile insult, but not because he considered *her* honorable. The need to defend and protect was simply hardwired into his being. He didn't trust her. Had absolutely no faith in her. And he never would.

The tears stung, but she'd had years of practice fighting them back. "You're not even going to give me a chance to explain."

The old feeling of helplessness, of abandonment, came rushing back. First Thomas, then her father. And now Hunter.

His face was so rigid she feared it would crack. "I came to find you because I missed you."

The stinging tears grew sharp, and her every breath felt heavy, as if she were breathing against a thick mask. "I came here to find some answers," she said, her voice thick with emotion. "Because I love yo—"

"Don't." He bit out the word so sharply it startled a nearby

guest, and he stepped closer, towering over her, his voice low. "Don't say it," he ground out.

Heart pounding, she froze, trying to find her voice again. "Hunter, I didn't learn a thing. I told you. I wanted to know the truth, and since you wouldn't tell me—"

"You want to hear what happened? Okay," he said, crossing his arms, his face hardly the picture of acceptance. "On the record, so you can use it to your heart's content and impress your boss with your in-depth knowledge."

Carly's soul curled up tighter, bled a little harder.

Hunter either didn't notice or didn't care. "I was used by a woman until she got what she wanted and left. I don't know if Mandy hooked up with me with that intention or not. I suspect my job simply pricked her interest and she decided to see where it led. But ultimately the story was more important than our relationship."

Despite her own pain, she hated the blank look on his face. "I'm sorry."

Hunter went on, ignoring her attempt at offering sympathy. "She wrote an article that revealed protected information about a cybercrime ring affiliated with the mob in Chicago. Information only our department knew. I'd been working on the case for two years, and I suspect she used a friend of mine from work—an FBI consultant—as her source. All I know is that it wasn't me," he said. Defeat joined forces with the anger in his voice and his lips twisted wryly, his bitter humor black. "But you can't prove a negative. And while a lack of evidence protects you from charges, it doesn't protect you from your colleagues' opinions." Hunter raked a hand through his hair, leaving it spiked on the top. "So I could have stayed and kept my job with restricted access, but I'd lost my zest for the work. Making money in a consulting business seemed the better option."

Her heart ached for him—the honorable man being accused. "I am not going to use the story," she said.

He continued as if she hadn't spoken. "Or maybe you need a little more blood and guts to really impact the reader?" He hiked a brow loaded with bitterness. "Like how devastating it was to be used by a woman I loved. How humiliating it was to be accused of putting the case I'd bled for at risk. The FBI was more than just a job. It was my life." He turned and headed for the bank of elevators.

Carly followed him. "I told you, I'm not printing a word."

Clearly unmoved by her words, he glanced down at her as he kept walking. "You forget I know how badly you want to prove to your father you've earned your stripes back." Reaching the elevators, he stepped inside one, turning to hold the doors open with his hands—blocking her entry. "So try this on for size, Carly," he said, looming over her. "You are a remarkable woman, but you should be less concerned about your father's opinion of you and more about your own. You can't earn your dad's respect until you grow up, act like an adult and develop a little respect for yourself." His gaze was relentless. "And that includes refraining from hopping from one loser's bed to the next."

Her hand connected with his cheek with a loud slap, but the sting in her palm was nothing compared to the pain in her heart. The words had landed too close to home. The last sliver of hope shriveled and died, and her words rasped out, heavy with a furious sarcasm. "As opposed to someone like you," she said, holding his gaze. "Well, here's a newsflash for you, Mr. Philips. You don't hold a monopoly on fidelity, bravery or *integrity*." Livid, frustrated he was taking the wounds from his past out on her, she bit out, "One judgmental man in my life is enough, so you can take your paternalistic attitude and go to hell."

His expression didn't ease. "That's not a problem," he said. "Because I expect more from the woman I love."

Carly's heart soared even as the floor dropped out from beneath her stomach, the twin sensations leaving her sick. The sting in her eyes grew sharper, because the horrible part was she knew it was true. She'd felt the emotion when he'd clung to her in the hotel room. Hunter *did* love her. But she also realized why that news didn't bring the happiness she'd always dreamed it would.

Because there were all kinds of love. The unrequited kind, that often left one bitter. The kind that was reciprocated, sure and strong, which made a person feel invincible. And then there was the kind that was returned but wasn't mature enough to last, stunted by the shadows of the past.

And that was what she had with Hunter.

"I expected more from the man *I* love," she said. Hunter's expression remained walled up as she went on. "I need a man who'll stick by my side. Who has faith in me." She fisted her hands at her side. "I need someone who *believes* in me."

His voice was dangerously soft. "Unfortunately," he said as he straightened up to push the elevator button, "that man isn't me."

Stricken, Carly stared at Hunter's *over you* expression as the elevator door closed, cutting off the excruciating view.

CHAPTER ELEVEN

"LIFE sucks." Carly flopped back onto the plush comforter of the king size bed in the hotel room, staring up at the ceiling.

Abby shot her a sympathetic look. "I don't think Hunter meant the things that he said, Carly."

Carly dragged the back of her hand across her eyes, impatient with herself. She was tired of being madder than hell. And she was equally fatigued from feeling as if Hunter had whipped out a gun and blasted a shot at her chest at close range, leaving her bleeding in the wake of his retreat. Since he'd packed up and left, gallantly paying the bill for an extra day—as if she'd *want* to stay and gamble her money when she'd already lost her heart—she'd fought back the urge to hunt him down. To knock that dumb metaphorical white hat off of his head, stomping on it until it was good and flat.

The exhaustive flip-flopping of her emotions had left her wrung out and empty.

Abby sat on the bed beside Carly. "Look at it this way," Abby said. She placed a comforting hand on Carly's shoulder and crinkled her brow, the jet-black pigtails shifting in response. "He wouldn't have been so upset about finding you talking to his old colleague if he didn't really care about you."

Care? He'd *said* he loved her. For years she'd dreamed of hearing those words from someone she loved in return, but she'd never imagined that the moment could bring such agony.

"I don't know," Carly said. Which was true. She didn't know anything anymore.

"Well…" The doubt on her friend's face was hardly encouraging. "He decked that guy for the comment he made about you." Her overly bright smile looked forced, and it was painful to watch. "That has to mean something."

"It means he found an excuse to do what he's probably wanted to do for years, using *my* supposed honor as an excuse." Carly rolled onto her stomach and buried her face in her arms. Her voice was muffled, which made going on easier—because the next set of words were the hardest she'd ever formed. "Except he doesn't see me as honorable."

"You love him," Abby said softly.

Spoken out loud, the words doubled Carly's misery, and the weight of the monstrous entity was a burden that threatened to drown her.

Carly turned her head on her arms, looking up at Abby. "You said it yourself. These things rarely work out."

"Sometimes they do," Abby said. "You just have to believe that they will."

With monumental effort, Carly briefly pushed aside her pain and stared up at her friend. She wasn't sure which was harder: enduring the expected pessimism while lost in a mire of hopeless misery, or the bud of hope that was now emanating from her friend's face. "Since when have you been a love convert?"

Guilt flickered through Abby's eyes. "Since I got married."

The words lingered in the air and gradually seeped into Carly's consciousness, her eyelids slowly stretching wide as the news settled deeper. It took a moment for the rest of her body to respond. When it did, she shot up, kneeling on the bed. "Married?"

"Pete and I visited a chapel on the strip yesterday," she said with a smile. "Elvis officiated."

Blinking hard, Carly tried to reconcile the pessimistic, down-on-relationships woman she knew with the glowing, almost upbeat woman in front of her. Happiness for her deserving friend and sadness for herself combined to overwhelm her, and she leaned forward, gathering Abby in a fierce hug. "I'm so pleased for you," she said, her throat clogged with emotion. Carly closed her eyes, resisting the urge to burst into tears. This would hardly be the I'm-happy-for-you moment her friend must have envisioned.

Abby held her tight. "One day I'll return the sentiment."

Carly didn't have the heart to rain on her friend's newfound joy, so she said nothing. The words that wanted to form were all negative. She had no clue how to tell her boss the truth about Hunter without losing her job. She had no idea how to heal the rift with her father, especially now that she'd screwed up again. And, worse, she was sure she'd never recover from loving Hunter. Though the word "recover" was probably better suited to catastrophic events.

Well, as far as Carly was concerned, love ranked right up there with floods, hurricanes and other natural disasters.

Abby pulled back, holding Carly's arms. "What are you going to do now?"

Carly knew her colleague was referring to more than just Hunter, and she pressed her lips together, potential answers swirling in her brain. Run away? Leave everything behind and start all over again? It was tempting, but it hadn't helped her three years ago when she'd come limping back home. And it hardly seemed the best solution now.

Gathering her resolve, she met her newly married friend's gaze with as much confidence as she could muster. "I'm going back to fix what I can." She blew out a shaky breath. "Starting with my dad."

Carly turned into the long, oak-tree-lined driveway of her childhood home, half wishing it would extend forever and she could avoid what waited for her at the end. She could just drive on indefinitely, enjoying the sunshine and the song on the radio, pretending her life was okay. Moving toward the moment of truth, or one of them anyway, but without having to actually face her father.

Nice try, Carly.

She was exhausted from the trip home and missing Hunter like she'd never thought possible. No easy-breezy forty-eight hour recovery this time. Honestly, she wasn't sure forty-eight *years* would lessen the pain. But it was time to tell her father what had happened. She hadn't just screwed up again— would probably get fired *again*—this time she'd also lost the one man she'd ever loved in the process. So...not only had she managed to repeat past mistakes, she'd gone and topped her previous efforts.

What father wouldn't be proud of such an accomplishment?

Carly's lips twisted at the grim irony as she parked in the drive and stared up at the massive colonial house, hoping to find a little courage in the view. It hadn't always been associated with unpleasant memories. Her childhood had been as happy as it could be, given she'd been minus a mother and her tiny two-person family was all she'd ever known. They'd muddled through contentedly enough until she'd hit puberty. But she could no longer afford to be the resentful adolescent who'd felt inadequate and misunderstood, and it was time to let the hurt go. Time for her to stop stubbornly waiting for her father to apologize and take the first step toward reconciliation.

Because it was either forgive him for letting her down or give up on their relationship forever.

She briefly pressed her lids together, seeking a happier place, and then exited, closing the car door with a determined thunk—praying her resolve was strong enough to withstand the next few minutes. Losing her newfound sense of inner peace at the first test was hardly the new and improved, more mature Carly she was striving to be.

A few minutes later she found her father under the back brick portico, standing next to one of the giant pillars that faced the Atlantic. He looked as if he'd aged since last week. And, despite her obstinate refusal to move on, she wasn't getting any younger either.

"Dad," she said, and then hesitated, at a loss what to say next.

He turned, and she braced, waiting for one of the subtle sarcastic slurs he always tossed in her direction. Or maybe she was the one who fired first, in an effort to beat him to it. Perhaps they'd taken turns. She couldn't remember. Either way, it always ended with one of them, or both, too angry to continue the conversation.

Two stubborn people stuck in the same behavioral pattern for years. In retrospect, given all she'd lost, it seemed petty and pointless.

His face was closed off and hardly welcoming. "Hello, kitten."

The stupid tears that lived just a heartbeat away bubbled to the surface, but she blinked them back. If he noticed, he didn't say anything. He simply turned and leaned a shoulder against the column, staring out over the Atlantic, while Carly struggled to find the right words.

It was a full minute before he said, "I was just thinking about that time you disguised yourself as a waitress at a party I threw for the mayor." He turned to study her. "How old were you? Sixteen? Seventeen?"

It wasn't the conversation she'd planned on having, and she certainly didn't relish the thought of rehashing old arguments. Dealing with the current ones seemed ambitious enough.

"Fifteen," she said. "You were so angry you grounded me for a month."

He shot her a sharp look. "I didn't have much choice."

"A month is forever to a fifteen-year-old."

"The mayor complained that you were *stalking* him at the gala."

She chewed on her lower lip before responding. "That wasn't entirely accurate," she said, debating the wisdom of sharing the truth. Carly shifted on her feet. "I was actually trying to question his wife about his mistress."

Her father's heavy eyebrows shot up in surprise as he let out a faintly amused scoff. "You never told me that."

She gave a small shrug. "I thought it best you didn't know."

"No wonder the mayor was so livid," he mused.

A pause followed, and Carly wasn't sure if he was amused by her stunt, impressed with her teenage chutzpah or annoyed by the memories of raising a frustratingly independent adolescent. And the closer she'd grown to adulthood, the more her father had been unhappy with his daughter's choices. Now that she was grown up, it seemed nothing she ever did measured up in his eyes. It was a bitter pill that sat in her stomach, refusing to dissolve.

His brow dug deep furrows. "Why are you here, Carly?"

"I need—" Her throat clamped hard, blocking the rest of her words, but she forced her feet to carry her closer to her father. She scanned the turquoise waters of the Atlantic. The late afternoon sun was sparkling on the surface and the salty breeze was balmy. The cold weather that had arrived when she'd first met Hunter had finally passed and moved on. Much like Hunter himself. Pain pierced her. His absence was like an empty chair at a crowded table, a constant reminder he'd walked away. But he'd been right. It was past time to deal with her father as an adult.

"I don't want to fight with you anymore," she said. She drew in a breath. "I know raising me wasn't easy."

A small frown slipped up his face and he looked uncomfortable with the topic—or maybe he was simply suspicious of her intentions. It was several seconds before he responded. "I run a multi-billion dollar company with hundreds of people on the payroll," he said, his voice a mixture of exasperation and defeat. "But I never knew how to handle you."

"I'm not a staff member to be managed, Dad," she said. "I'm your daughter."

He sent her an aggravated look. "Employees are easier."

"Yes, because you can simply dictate what you want." Carly sighed and crossed her arms. "People in *real* relationships don't respond well to the method."

He stared at her for what felt like forever, and then shook his head, looking a hundred years older than he should. "I'm sure your mother would have done a better job," he said, his face haggard.

The sting of tears returned. "I'm sorry I was a difficult teen."

"It's just…" He blew out a breath and rubbed a hand across his forehead, leaving the wild eyebrows in even more disarray. He caught her gaze with an almost urgent intensity. "I won't be around forever," he said, his voice firm yet sincere. "And one of these days your choices are going to get you into *real* trouble."

A dull ache thumped, and Carly pressed her fingers to her temples, hoping to ease the sudden pounding. "Okay," she went on reluctantly. "You were right. Thomas was using me." She dropped her hands to her side. "But I didn't love him," she said. That fact had been made abundantly clear when she fell in love with Hunter.

The constant free-falling feeling returned and fear froze

her chest, making its work difficult. For a moment she could scarcely breathe.

Damn. Love didn't just hurt. It *paralyzed*.

"I know," he said.

Surprise drew her brows together in confusion, but her father went on with a small wave of his hand.

"Oh, I didn't believe that you'd slept with the senator for the story any more than I believed the rumor you'd fallen in love with him and let your emotions cloud your objectivity. I knew better. And in some ways…" he shook his head with a grim look "…I almost wished the latter was true."

Shocked, she stared at him, her mouth gaping as she tried to make sense of the words. "I don't understand."

He heaved out another heavy breath. "At least then you would have risked your career for something more than a fascination for a man just because he'd been labeled an individualist."

Carly held still, absorbing the words that were hard to hear even as her father went on, serving up more of the same.

"And since then you've been in and out of a number of relationships. Most of the men weren't worthy of your time, but I wouldn't have cared so much if you'd actually *loved* one of them."

She opened her mouth to speak, but there were no words of defense. And so far love had yet to provide her that warm, fuzzy feeling that got paired with the condition. Since the moment those elevator doors had closed in her face, with Hunter's words haunting her, she'd started to wonder if her relationships since Thomas had been about avoiding the big L. Because Hunter's accusations had left her raw, bleeding, for the second time in her life—abandoned again, without the chance to explain herself. Her father hadn't wanted to hear her side three years ago, and Hunter didn't want to hear hers now.

But maybe her father was finally ready to listen.

"Thomas and I didn't start seeing one another until after the story was done," she said.

"I know that now." He paused, his frank expression brutally painful. "I wasn't as convinced back then."

It hurt to hear the truth and it seemed horribly unfair. But life wasn't fair, and maybe it was never meant to be. Regardless, it was up to her to handle herself, despite feeling she'd been wronged. And maybe that was the ultimate lesson.

The only control she had was over her own behavior.

"Carly," her father said, "when are you going to grow up and stop flitting from one guy to the next?"

Her heart wrenched, the pain stealing her breath. The time to come clean was now. Would he be happy to hear she'd finally fallen in love when he learned that in all probability her emotional development came at the cost of her job? Her boss had hired her despite her past, giving her the second chance that she'd just destroyed.

But the agony of losing Hunter put the threat in perspective.

"I've been asking my boss for approval to write a story on Hunter Philips." The tone in her voice must have held the warning that bad news was ahead, because her father looked as if he was bracing for the impact, and a little part of her heart died again. "She finally gave me the go-ahead, but..." Her voice stalled. She was too afraid to go on, dreading the look of disappointment in his face. Apparently her expression said it all.

"You've slept with him," he said, his face resigned.

Her heart clenched even as her stomach rolled. He eyed her steadily, and she wished she could read more beneath the weary acceptance.

"You can't do the story now," he said.

"I realize that."

"You have to tell your boss why."

"I realize that too."

Neither one of them spoke of the obvious.

Her throat so tight it was painful, she said, "I'm in love with him."

The expression on her face must have conveyed the massive ache in her heart, because her father didn't look happy for her. He looked like he was sharing her pain but wasn't sure what to do about it.

He took a hesitant step closer. "Carly…"

Letting the emotion wash through her, Carly crossed the last few feet, and he folded her awkwardly in his arms.

The hug was brief, but full of the familiar smell of the peppermints he loved, before he set her back. "I'm sorry he hurt you," her father said gruffly.

Conscious of his discomfort—her father would never be the touchy-feely sort—she tried to smile. She couldn't have her father thinking it was all Hunter's fault. She cleared her throat, clogged with unshed tears. "He's a good guy," she said. "An honorable one."

Too bad he couldn't believe she had the ability to be honorable too.

Her father raised a bushy eyebrow. "What are you going to tell your boss?"

She lifted her chin. "The truth," she said. And it was a good thing Hunter had pushed her to quit being stubborn about her dad, because she would need his support in the coming weeks. "I'm going to write the best damn profile piece I can on someone else and offer it as a replacement," she said, steadily meeting her father's gaze. "And then I'm going to go on Brian O'Connor's show, meet Hunter face to face, and finish what I started."

"Were you given a hard time when you backed out of tonight's Brian O'Connor show?" Booker asked.

Jaw clenched, eyes on the three-foot-long punching bag hanging in the well-stocked gym of his home, Hunter swung with his right arm. His fist connected with a satisfying thwack. "Not really," he said. He did his best to ignore the digital clock on the wall.

11:44 p.m.

A sickening feeling rose, burning his chest and his gut, as Hunter went on. "There isn't anything left to debate." Except maybe his sanity, considering he'd had to learn the same lesson all over again.

He landed another solid punch, forcing back the urge to pummel the bag in frustration, knowing Booker was waiting for him to say more. But Hunter was washed out, too tired from his workout—and the current state of his life—to engage in much conversation.

The week since he'd arrived home from Las Vegas had been busy, consumed by a job that at one time had seemed perfect. Hunter had managed to carve out some time to explore the idea he'd formulated after Carly had questioned his career priorities. But after all that had happened, dealing with Carly on live TV again went beyond his abilities. Surviving this evening, knowing she'd be on the air without him, was proving to be tough.

It would take a miracle to get through the next quarter of an hour without losing his mind, or his resolve *not* to watch the show. Hunter glanced at the clock.

11:45.

Hunter began to pummel the bag, the repeated thumps filling the silence until his friend spoke again.

"It's on in fifteen minutes," Booker said, as if every cell in Hunter's body wasn't acutely aware of that fact. "Are you gonna watch?"

Hunter's abdomen clenched as if hit. His chest and arm muscles burned from his intense workout, but in a way the pain was an improvement. Since his argument with Carly he'd moved through his days in a trancelike state. Numb. Anesthetized. Trying hard to forget the maddening sight of Carly talking with Terry.

And the devastated look on her face as the elevator doors had closed…

With a hard jab, Hunter's fist met the bag, jarring his left arm. But the sensation did nothing to ease the conflicting images in his head.

"Because I think you should tune in to see what she says," Booker went on.

"No." Hunter punctuated the word with a mighty slug. "I'm not watching the show."

Public curiosity had swelled since he'd backed out forty-eight hours ago. True to form, Carly hadn't canceled her commitment to appear. Whether she'd stuck with it for the publicity, or for some other reason, he wasn't sure. But he'd seen the advertisement announcing the replacement topic: the debut of Carly Wolfe's new series. A column spotlighting a different Miami resident every week. She'd finally reached her goal.

The question was, who had she chosen as her first subject?

The clock on the wall read 11:47, and bile rose in the back of his throat. His stomach churned at the thought of watching her discuss everything he'd vomited out in a fit of anger. Muscles coiled tight, he felt the dark potential twine its way around his limbs. He refused to watch as the woman he loved traded in all they'd shared to achieve the career goal she'd chased for three years.

The familiar feeling of betrayal, the boil of resentment, left him battering the stuffed leather bag with a one-two punch that jarred him all the way to his soul.

"I find this situation very interesting," Booker said. "I'm usually the one who sees a conspiracy at every turn."

Hunter raised a wry eyebrow at Booker. "Are you saying I'm being paranoid, like you?"

His shaggy brown hair was in need of a trim, and Booker's smile was wide as he brushed his bangs back. "Your suspicions don't involve whole nations and large governmental agencies. So, compared to me, you're small-time." His voice changed to a more serious note. "But you *are* skeptical of everything that moves, Hunt." He paused before going on. "And I think you're wrong about Carly."

Pushing aside the crushing doubt made worse by Booker's chastising expression, Hunter shot his partner a doubtful look. "Of course you'd say that. You married her best friend," Hunter said. He was still trying to adjust to *that* particular turn of events.

"Abby and I decided it would be better for our relationship if we didn't discuss you two."

"Smart move. Still, you might be biased."

"Or I might be right."

Hunter's chest clamped hard, squeezing with a grip so tight it made breathing and circulating his blood a mammoth chore. His heart still managed to pump the lingering fear to the far reaches of his body. Fear that he'd learn he'd screwed up the one good thing to happen to him in so long that he hadn't recognized it for what it was…

Real. Genuine. And built to last.

With a silent curse, Hunter closed his eyes. The last time he'd made love to Carly his heart had claimed it was legit. That she was on the up and up. But he'd taken one look at her talking to Terry and his heart had taken a sharp U-turn. All the old suspicions, the duplicities of the past, had come screaming back. The avalanche of anger, humiliation, the need for self-preservation had plowed into him with a force that had swept him up in its wake.

If Carly hadn't run the story he'd accused her of going after, what then?

He opened his eyes and began punching the bag again, the lingering question feeding the massive knot growing in his chest.

Hunter was saved from dwelling on the unbearable thought when his friend spoke.

"Is it back to business as usual, then?" Booker said.

Hunter stopped punching and turned to face his friend and business partner. Regardless of the outcome tonight, the status quo had changed. He couldn't continue to pretend his life was enjoyable. Actually, it wasn't even tolerable. Making money hand over clenched fist wasn't good enough anymore. It was time to come clean about his plans.

"I had a long talk with the special agent in charge of the Miami division of the FBI," Hunter said. With a look of surprise, Booker crossed his arms and leaned against the wall, clearly settling in to hear more. "They're very interested in help with their caseload," Hunter said, steadily meeting Booker's gaze as he went on. "I signed on to become a part-time consultant."

A few moments passed, and then a smile slowly crept up Booker's face. "Catching the criminals was always your specialty."

Relieved Booker understood, Hunter delivered the rest of his news as matter-of-factly as he could. "Which means I'm going to need more help in the day-to-day running of the business."

Booker didn't hesitate. "Not a problem."

Narrowing his eyes, he wondered if his friend understood exactly what he was asking. "I thought you hated dealing with the clients."

The pause lasted long enough for his partner's face to take

on a guarded look. His words were cautious. "You set some pretty high standards, Hunt," Booker said.

Hunter stared at his friend, the implication of the statement washing over him as Booker swiped a hand through his shaggy hair again and went on.

"I hate feeling as if I'm not doing a good enough job."

Stunned, Hunter stared at his friend. "Did I give you that impression?"

"Not directly. But you're a hard act to follow," he said. "And you're fairly demanding when it comes to your expectations."

The possibility that Booker had been avoiding clients for a reason outside his social discomfort had never occurred to Hunter. Booker's voice dropped, and Hunter got a disturbing feeling the topic had widened to include more than just work.

"Sometimes you hold the people in your life to pretty impossible standards," Booker said.

Hunter's throat constricted so tight swallowing was impossible. He glanced at the clock on the wall.

11:55.

Booker picked up the remote control to the flatscreen TV mounted on the wall, holding it out to Hunter. "Do yourself a favor, Hunt," Booker said. "Watch the show."

Heart thudding loudly in his chest, Hunter removed his gloves and took the remote. Without another word, his friend headed for the exit.

Hunter stared at the black TV screen for a full four minutes, the digital numbers on the clock marking the passage of time, minute by agonizing minute. Either way, he had to know. He just wasn't sure which would be worse. Losing Carly as a result of her actions…or *his.*

Finally, unable to take the tension any longer, he pushed the "on" button and flipped to the right channel. His fifty-eight inch TV was filled with the image of Carly sitting on

Brian O'Connor's couch. Beautiful, of course, in a gauzy top and skirt. But the sight of her lovely legs, glossy brunette hair, and warm, amber-colored eyes was nothing compared to the shock he got when the camera panned to the right. Sitting next to her were two young adults in typical urban street clothes. Thad and Marcus. The two graffiti artists she'd been interviewing that day in the alley. The first Miami residents to be featured in her new series. Not him, after all, then.

Hell.

Nausea boiled, his chest burned, and Hunter gripped the leather punching bag to steady himself, his mind churning with memories. The vile words from his mouth. The stricken expression on Carly's face. She'd said she needed a man who trusted her. A man who had faith in her. Who *believed* in her. He'd screwed up royally at the very moment he'd confessed he loved her.

So how could he ever convince her now?

CHAPTER TWELVE

DESPITE the ebony-colored tablecloths with their center-pieces consisting of dried dead roses, the ambiance on the restaurant's outdoor patio was festive. Carly was amazed that Pete and Abby had managed to find the perfect balance of Gothic and elegance to celebrate their recent marriage. Lit by candlelight that reflected off the blanket of fog covering the terrace floor, the evening was cast in an otherworldly glow. Waiters circulated, their platters laden with appetizers. Guests ordered drinks at two beautiful mahogany bars, crafted to resemble coffins. Or maybe they were real. If so, Carly hoped the caskets were new.

In jeans, sneakers and a black T-shirt, Pete Booker cast his wife of two weeks an adoring look, and Carly's heart tripped over a mix of envy and happiness.

Standing beside her, her father muttered, "This is the strangest wedding reception I've ever been to." He dubiously eyed a discreetly placed fog machine before turning his gaze to the bride's outfit.

Abby's black long-sleeved gloves were paired with a matching corset dress that flared into a full-length lace skirt, trailing to the floor with a Victorian flare and a Gothic attitude.

Carly's lips twitched in amusement. "Thanks for coming with me, Dad." She clutched the strap of her silver beaded evening purse, running a hand down her halter-top dress of midnight satin. It wasn't her usual choice, but all the guests had been requested to wear black. At least the color suited her mood. "I hated the thought of showing up alone."

"Yeah…" Her dad let out an awkward harrumph and shifted on his feet. "Well…" he went on uneasily, and Carly's mouth twitched harder.

"Don't worry," she said. "I won't start crying again."

Her dad sent her a look loaded with fear. "Please don't."

Carly almost laughed. She had rallied and poured on the charm for the final show, but when it was done she'd fallen apart—and her father had barely survived the onslaught of tears. She'd finally come to realize her dad did not handle a crying woman well—something she hadn't fully understood until now. He would never be the perfect parent, ready with an understanding hug, a reassuring smile and gentle words of wisdom. Then again, she was hardly the perfect daughter, either. But he was here tonight, supporting her in his own way. And for that she was inordinately grateful.

Because eventually Hunter would make an appearance.

Anxiety settled deep. If she ever decided to date again— like maybe a million years from now—she was going to give her choice more serious thought. Both for her sake and the man's. Hunter might have been protecting himself by throwing up walls, but outside of Carly at least he hadn't hurt anyone in the process. She, on the other hand, had left a trail of unhappy boyfriends in her wake.

All of them had deserved better than her pathetic attempts to stick with men who had no hope of capturing her heart.

When she spied Hunter heading in her direction, said heart sputtered to a stop, and she reached out to grasp the back of a nearby chair. After a few earth-shaking seconds she pushed away the budding, soul-sucking vortex of gloom.

Her father glanced at Hunter and then shot her a worried look. "Do you want me to stay?" he asked, almost as if he hoped she'd say no. "Or do you want me to fetch you a drink?"

She was tempted to keep him around as a shield. But she'd made a pact with herself today that there would be no more wallowing.

She tried for a reassuring smile. "Drink, please," she said to her father. With a deep breath, she straightened her shoulders and met Hunter's gaze as he strode through the crowd in her direction. "I'm going to need it," she muttered.

Her dad headed for a casket lined with bottles, shooting Hunter a glare infused with a good bit of concern.

Hunter came to a stop a few feet from her. In an impeccably cut black suit, he looked as handsome and intimidating as ever—every muscle poised, prepared for battle. His cool slate-blue eyes were trained on her face. But this time his hair was spiked in front, as if he'd run an impatient hand through it multiple times. A brief flicker of uncertainty came and went, replaced with his usual determined gaze.

It took several moments and more than a few blinks of her eyelids to jumpstart her heart again. His presence had robbed her of her earlier confidence, so she'd just have to fake it until her mojo returned for real.

"I came to tell you I spoke with Booker and we're all square," he said carefully, his eyes probing, as if testing her response. "We've worked out a plan for me to put in some time doing consulting work for the FBI."

She refused to be swayed by the news. "Glad to hear it."

Neither mentioned their parting words at the elevator, but the ghost of their painful falling-out hung in the air, as if lurking in the fog-blanketed shadows. His eyes held hers, and the determined focus, the sense of purpose radiating from his face, made her heart work harder.

After a tension-filled pause, he said, "Congratulations on

your new series too. How did you get your boss to agree to your plans for your column?"

"I didn't sleep with her, if that's what you're suggesting."

A small smile appeared, more sad than amused. "It's not."

"I confessed everything, and then handed her a story on Thad and Marcus that blew her socks off."

His tone broadcast just how pleased he was. "Good for you."

"Yeah," she said. Just for good measure, she hiked her chin higher. "Go, me." Smart words, in retrospect. Because right about now leaving sounded like a wise plan. She'd missed him, had ached for him, but he also brought a host of sharp emotions along with the longing. Ultimately, it was the confusion and pain that drove her away. "Well…" She cleared her throat, the sound awkward. "I should find my dad." She turned on her heel.

He put his hand on her arm to stop her, his touch setting off all kinds of alarms. "I shouldn't haven't insulted you," he said, the regret in his eyes profound. "I'm sorry."

Ignoring the feel of his fingers on her skin, she took a deep breath, glad the initial icy tension was broken. His apology didn't make up for not believing in her, but it helped ease the ending. "I shouldn't have slapped you," she said with a tiny sheepish shrug. "It was an impulse reaction."

"I deserved it."

Oh, dear God, it was the agreeable Hunter from the first show. The one who was so hard to argue with. The one who knew how to work her to get just what he wanted, whether it be irritation, confessing her deepest doubts…or a sensual surrender.

The question was, what did he want now?

"Hunter," she said with a sigh, pulling her arm away. "I think we've said everything there is to say." Like he might love her, but didn't really know how. Not in the way she needed. The sharp ache resurfaced.

"I'm not finished," he said. "I wanted to tell you I spent the last week trying to perfect my new app."

She frowned, confused. "I don't care about—"

"Marry me," he said bluntly.

She sucked in a breath, feeling the hit, and her stomach clamped into a knot.

She shot him a look, trying to hide her weakening resolve. "You show up, after all this time, and just expect me to accept your proposal? It's been *seven days* since you left me high and dry on the TV show, and—"

"I had some work to do before I could face you."

She lifted an incredulous brow. "You confronted two men in a dangerous Miami alley, yet you couldn't deal with me face to face?"

"Not after the mistake that I'd made."

They'd both made several, and it was more than a few rapid heartbeats that passed before she was able to respond. When she did, the word came out soft. "Coward."

His lips twisted grimly. "In some things, yes."

Put an innocent in harm's way and he would bravely confront the most fearsome of opponents. But when faced with an emotional risk he cut and ran. It was a truth she needed to remember, despite the fact he was here now…looking wonderful…and her body was remembering the advantage of making love to a man with a fighter's muscles…her heart was remembering how the action-hero defender made her feel.

Protected. *Loved.*

Gathering her wits, she shifted her gaze away, blinking hard to maintain her composure. The guests were lining up at the unusual wedding cake: a six-tiered confection of white icing thick with a thorny trimming done in black. Carly tried to imagine taking the marital leap with Hunter, waiting for him to walk out…

"I can't marry you," she said. And with as much grace as she could muster, she headed for the bar and her father.

Halfway there her cellphone chirped, and she pulled it from her purse and opened the message. The soulful sounds of the song "Share My Life" crooned from her phone, and the screen filled with the words "Marry Me."

She gripped her cellular, her stomach settling on top of her toes. She hadn't recovered from the first proposal, and now he was sending a second. Another proposal that left her confused, doubting her resolve to be strong. Fingers shaky, she selected "No" and scrolled through the list of rejection songs to accompany her response. There were only ten. With feeling, she firmly jabbed the button next to "Love Stinks."

From behind her, the reedy sound of the song filled the air.

Carly whirled around to face Hunter, and his gaze held hers as he crossed closer, coming to a stop in front of her.

Now that she knew his plan, her whole body was filled with caution. "You *have* been busy."

"Designing the app is the easy part. Finding the right songs is hard." He eyed her levelly as he said, "I also discontinued The Ditchinator."

She gave him no leeway with her expression and she forced herself to maintain eye contact, desperately trying to calm her nerves. But she tipped her head, her voice reflecting her curiosity. "Why?"

His eyes held hers with conviction. "Because you wanted me to."

Feeling raw, Carly fought the urge to get misty-eyed. He'd done it to make her happy.

"I also decided you'd prefer something more positive," he said. "So I replaced The Ditchinator with The Hitchinator."

At the name, humor briefly overrode the angst, and her

mouth worked, biting back a smile. "Your new app needs a lot of work," she said, as lightly as she could, but all her doubts made it a tough sell. "The Hitchinator is a bit of a retreaded name, and the selection of music to accompany a refusal is pretty limited."

He tipped his head meaningfully. "But there are thirty ways to say yes."

"Do you think it will sell well?"

"I'm only worried about winning over one customer." His voice dropped a notch. "You."

Her heart pounded out its approval even as she struggled to remain strong.

"I didn't expect you to say yes...the first time," he said, taking a half-step closer.

She ignored the chaotic pumping in her chest, the surge of heat in her veins. The longing that went beyond the physical and traveled all the way to her soul. She forced herself to maintain his gaze, though her heart and her heated blood screamed *retreat*. To end the torture of continuing to tell him no.

"I should go find my father," she said, and turned and headed in the direction of her dad at the bar.

Ten feet from her intended destination, her safe haven, another chirp came from her cellphone. She stopped mid-step and glanced at her cellular with a powerful blend of dread... and hope. She pressed the button and the words "Marry Me" reappeared. The phone vibrated to the tune of Billy Idol's "White Wedding." Carly couldn't restrain the small bark of laughter. When the humor passed, again she pushed "No" and scrolled through the rejection choices, choosing one. But this time her fingers hovered hesitantly for several seconds. Biting her lip, she pushed "send."

Her selection of "Bad Romance" filled the air, coming from *directly* behind her, and Carly closed her eyes.

Don't let him charm you, Carly.

But her heart felt more vulnerable when she turned to face Hunter, standing just three feet from her. She gripped the strap of her purse. How could she survive this encounter when he was so close, looking and smelling wonderful and depriving her of her ability to breathe?

"Did you think Billy Idol's 'White Wedding' would endear me to your cause?" she said, knowing he knew it had.

"The first song was too obvious. And I know how much you love the unexpected," he said. "Besides…" He looked at a nearby table topped with an ornate haunted-house style candelabra, flickering in the night. "I've seen the video. 'White Wedding' seemed appropriate, given our current setting."

"Hunter—"

"I'm sorry I didn't believe you," he interrupted firmly, his eyes intense.

Her heart knocked faster, begging to be set free from its self-imposed cage, and panic squeezed Carly's chest. "Too little, too late," she said. "Before the last show I was hoping you'd turn up and say you'd changed your mind. That you trusted me and didn't need any proof beyond your belief in me." She stared at him, dwelling on those painful days. "An apology would have meant something *before* you had evidence I was telling the truth."

A host of emotions filtered across his face before landing on regret. "I know."

With a single finger he touched her hand, and her heart rattled the bars of its pen. But she fought the weakness and her growing doubts as he went on.

"I'm hoping you'll accept my apology anyway," he said. "And I'd be even more pleased if you'd agree to marry me."

Her throat ached as she fought back the tears and the overwhelming need to say *yes*. Good God, she was tired of crying. "Why should I?"

"Because I'd like a second chance." Her throat closed over completely, and when she didn't respond he continued. "I made a mistake," he said, his voice harsh with emotion. "But it doesn't mean I don't love you."

"I know you do," she said. "But Hunter—"

He opened his mouth to cut her off again, but Carly placed her fingers on his lips, stopping his words.

Shifting her gaze between two beautiful slate-blue eyes, she said in a low voice, "I can't live my life walking on eggshells, worrying that I might do or say something that shakes your trust in me again." She ignored the intense heat in his gaze and the feel of his lips, the unyielding softness that was oh, so uniquely Hunter. Her chest caught, and breathing became difficult. She dropped her arm, gathering the courage to continue. "All because you can't move on."

"I can," he fired off in a low voice. He shifted closer, towering over her, his tone softening. "Give me a second chance to prove it."

She still hadn't heard a good enough reason. "Why should I?" she repeated.

His words tumbled out. "Because I let my fear push you away," he said gruffly. Face frustrated, he raked a hand through his hair and looked across the crowded terrace. The pause felt like forever, but when he finally turned back, his expression was frank. Raw.

The last barrier was gone.

"I knew you loved me," he said, his words rough, heavy with the truth. "But I didn't trust the feeling and I was too scared to believe you. I don't deserve another chance. But I'm asking anyway," he said. "Because I'm tired of being unhappy and alone. All because I'm a gutless coward."

As if taking a moment to collect himself, he dropped his gaze to her bare shoulder and brushed her hair back, leaving a skitter of goosebumps. His hand settled between her

shoulder blades, cupping her skin as if it planned to stay. He
lifted his eyes to hers, and the brutal honesty stole what little
composure she had left.

"And I think fear is driving your decisions now," he said.

Her mind balked at the idea and she hiked her chin, forcing the tears away with a watery sniff. "I am *not* scared."

The words sounded hollow even to her own ears.

Several seconds ticked by, and though his gaze was intense
there was a touch of humor mixed with a hint of desperation.
His voice, however, was pure daring conviction. "Then mar-
rying me shouldn't be a problem."

As his warm palm cradled her back, Carly's heart thumped
loudly in her chest, reinforcing the message that he could have
called her a coward too, but hadn't. Or that he *could* have insisted he was right, which he was.

Despite everything, she sent him a suspicious look. "Are
you *daring* me to marry you?"

"The woman I love never walks away from a challenge."

Her lips twisted into a self-directed frustrated frown.
"Damn it," she said in a low tone. "I hate that you're right."

The happy sounds of chatter filled the air as his eyes continued to scan hers in a question, stripping her to the emotional bone. Until he said, "So, Carly Wolfe, which would
you rather have?" Despite the words, in spite of the teasing
light in his eyes, his tone was serious. "A life with me, learning how to do love right, or an endless succession of singing
break-up telegrams?"

The question—and the skin-on-skin touch on her back—
made breathing difficult. Which wasn't so good for formu-
lating complicated responses. Fortunately the answer was
simple. "You," she finally said. "I choose you."

Relief, joy and fire flashed in his eyes, and with a
lightning-fast movement, Hunter hauled her against him. Her

body collided with his and she sighed, her heart melting as she curled into his embrace.

His chest was hard. Protective.

The hand on her back was warm. And gentle.

Sandwiched between the perfect combination of unyielding strength and soothing comfort, she inhaled his familiar woodsy scent. The surge of happiness overwhelmed her and she buried her face against him, his soft jacket absorbing the embarrassing wet tracks on her cheek.

After a minute, Hunter said, "Just promise me something."

She slid her arms around his waist, blinked back the remaining tears and looked up at him. "Anything."

He glanced at the two coffin bars surrounded by guests dressed in black, their feet obscured by the mist from the fog machines. "No Elvis at the wedding," he said. "And no Goth-themed receptions."

Finally allowing herself to trust the joy, she let a smile creep up her face. "Can I ask the winner of the Pink Flamingo drag queen pageant to officiate?"

Hunter's eyes briefly flickered wider—but to his credit he said nothing.

She lifted an eyebrow. "Now who's afraid?"

"Good point," he said, his brow creased in humor, his fingers caressing her skin.

"So, tell me…" Her mojo firmly back in place, she flashed him her most charming smile and tipped her head curiously. "What kind of songs does The Hitchinator offer when I accept your proposal?"

A secretive smile spread across his face, and the light in his slate-blue eyes grew warmer. "I'll resend the message so you can hit 'Yes' and find out."

* * * * *

A sneaky peek at next month...

MODERN™

INTERNATIONAL AFFAIRS, SEDUCTION & PASSION GUARANTEED

My wish list for next month's titles...

In stores from 15th June 2012:

❏ The Secrets She Carried – Lynne Graham
❏ Heart of a Desert Warrior – Lucy Monroe
❏ A Royal World Apart – Maisey Yates
❏ The Count's Prize – Christina Hollis

In stores from 6th July 2012:

❏ To Love, Honour and Betray – Jennie Lucas
❏ Unnoticed and Untouched – Lynn Raye Harris
❏ Distracted by her Virtue – Maggie Cox
❏ The Tarnished Jewel of Jazaar – Susanna Carr
❏ Keeping Her Up All Night – Anna Cleary

Available at WHSmith, Tesco, Asda, Eason, Amazon and Apple

Just can't wait?

0612/01

Special Offers

Every month we put together collections and longer reads written by your favourite authors.

Here are some of next month's highlights— and don't miss our fabulous discount online!

On sale 15th June

On sale 15th June

On sale 6th July